LAST MINUTE ROMANCE

Etta Sanderson has to fly to Turkey unexpectedly to help Kaan Talbot guide a group of tourists around the country. At first Kaan resents her inexperience, but they begin to appreciate each other's abilities. When they discover that some of the tourists are using the trip as a cover for criminal activities, Kaan and Etta work together to frustrate their schemes — but despite this success, is it too soon to think of planning a future together?

SHEILA HOLROYD

LAST MINUTE ROMANCE

Complete and Unabridged

LINFORD
Leicester

First published in Great Britain in 2012

First Linford Edition
published 2013

British Library CIP Data

Holroyd, Sheila.
  Last minute romance. - -
  (Linford romance library)
  1. Love stories.
  2. Large type books.
  I. Title II. Series
  823.9′2–dc23

  ISBN 978–1–4448–1468–2

Published by
F. A. Thorpe (Publishing)
Anstey, Leicestershire

Set by Words & Graphics Ltd.
Anstey, Leicestershire
Printed and bound in Great Britain by
T. J. International Ltd., Padstow, Cornwall

This book is printed on acid-free paper

1

As Etta made her way through the Istanbul airport gate she saw a small group of travellers clustered together in the near-deserted arrivals hall. She hurried towards them, smiling nervously and dragging her two suitcases behind her. In front of the group stood a tall, dark-haired young man who was frowning deeply and holding up a notice announcing 'Top Turkish Tours'.

Etta came to a halt in front of him. 'I'm sorry,' she said breathlessly. 'I didn't know about the visa, you see, and it took me ages to sort it out.'

The young man was looking past her at the gate, as if expecting someone else to appear, but he spared her a quick, impatient, glance.

'I'm afraid you've got the wrong group. All my clients are here.' He looked back at the gate and his frown grew even blacker. 'Did you notice if there was anybody else waiting to come through?'

'Not that I saw.' She dropped her shoulder bag. 'Oh! Are you looking for Harry Sayers?'

Now she suddenly had his full attention.

'Yes, I am, as a matter of fact. How do you know?'

Etta smiled and held out her hand. 'I'm Etta Sanderson. Harry couldn't come, so I'm here instead. I'm afraid I don't know much about Turkey, but I'm sure I'll learn quickly.'

He stared at her in horror, ignoring her hand until she let it drop feebly to her side, her smile gradually fading.

'The travel agency has sent you instead of Harry? Somebody who doesn't know Turkey? They must be mad!' Then he gave a swift glance at the small group fidgeting behind him and gave an impatient sigh. 'You'd better come on, then. We'll sort things out back at the hotel.'

2

Suddenly his frown vanished as he turned to the waiting travellers, so that he appeared relaxed and smiling as he faced them. 'Well, it seems that we're all here at last, so let's go to the coach. It's waiting for us over there.'

Obediently the group began to haul their luggage in the direction he indicated. Etta waited for someone to offer to help her with her cases. In her experience, someone always volunteered if she looked helpless, but it didn't seem to work this time. The dark-haired young man, busy with an elderly lady, looked back at her and jerked his head towards the exit.

'Hurry up or you'll miss the coach!'

Reluctantly she began to pull her cases along as he led the way out of the airport building to a large coach, whose driver sprang into action as the group appeared, rapidly loading all the cases into the storage area.

Etta handed over her luggage and then scrambled up the steps into the coach where she looked round, wondering where she should sit. The young man climbed on after her and wordlessly pointed at the front seat. Then, when he had seen the clients were all safely aboard, he sat beside her.

As the coach was driven out of the airport, the young man murmured to her that he had to give the usual introduction and stood up to address the passengers.

'Welcome to Turkey! My name is Kaan Talbot. K-A-A-N. I am your guide for the next few days. We shall soon be at your hotel where your rooms are waiting for you, and I am sure you are all ready for bed.'

He glanced at his watch. 'As you can see, it's nearly midnight already. I'm sorry for the delay at the airport.' His eyes rested briefly on Etta and she found herself blushing. 'As you know, we are leaving Istanbul early tomorrow, so I suggest you get as much sleep as possible before your six-thirty wake-up call.'

He paused while the passengers

groaned. 'There will be a short meeting in Reception at eight tomorrow morning when you will meet the other tour members and I will be able to give you all a little more information. Then we should be on our way by nine o'clock. Now I'll let you rest.'

He sat down again beside Etta, but spoke only to tell her that it would take about twenty minutes to reach the hotel.

When they arrived he ushered the tourists off the coach and into the reception area. Within ten minutes they had been checked in, offered coffee and sandwiches, and assured that their cases were being taken to their rooms.

When he had finished with the tourists Kaan Talbot turned to Etta as she waited for instructions, wondering what to do. 'Come with me. We'll get a coffee and then we'll sit over there.'

She followed him, yawning. It had been a very long day.

'First of all,' he started when they were seated, 'your tourist agency in

England was asked to send someone to come with me on this tour so they could appreciate what Top Turkish Tours has to offer. We specifically asked for someone experienced because we need to provide an efficient service. It was finally arranged that Harry would come because he has worked in Turkey as a travel rep before. I met him then and we became friends. Why isn't he here?'

'He was all ready to come, but then he tripped over something in the office early this morning and hurt his ankle so badly that he couldn't walk.'

Kaan sighed, and then nodded resignedly.

'I see. At least, I can see why Harry couldn't come, but why were you sent if you don't know anything about Turkey? Where else have you worked in travel?'

Etta shook her head a little forlornly.

'I've been working in the agency office for some months, although I haven't had any experience with clients actually on holiday. But I have been on holiday abroad several times,' she offered hopefully. However she had to admit that none of those holidays had been to Turkey.

'Then why on earth did they send you?' he demanded impatiently. 'There must have been someone more suitable.'

'Because by the time it was clear that Harry wouldn't be able to come, they only had an hour to find a replacement before it was time to leave for the airport!' she said with a touch of spirit. 'I was supposed to be going on holiday this afternoon straight from the office and so I was sitting there with my cases packed and my passport in my handbag. Under the circumstances, I volunteered to postpone my holiday to come here and everybody agreed it was the only solution.'

She looked at him angrily. Didn't he appreciate that she had sacrificed her holiday to help him? 'I know I need experience, and this is a way of getting it. I'll do my best.'

He drank his coffee and sighed resignedly. 'Have you any idea of what we have to do?'

She nodded eagerly. 'We have to take the tourists to various sites of interest and tell them all about them, then take them to the hotels.'

He closed his eyes in apparent despair. 'Do you have a notebook with you?'

'What for?'

'To make sure you have a record of all the little details that help to make sure that everyone enjoys their holiday — things like who has an allergy to a specific food, who has trouble climbing stairs, who wants decaffeinated coffee, for example.'

'Is all that necessary?'

'It is essential. It's not just a matter of attention to detail making for a better atmosphere. If we make sure they enjoy their holiday then they'll tell their friends and hopefully they will book with us in the future.' He sighed again. 'Well, we'll have to hope you're a very quick learner.'

He glanced at her from under lowered lashes. 'Incidentally, Miss Sanderson, as the hotel was expecting two male guides, they have given us a double room.'

He laughed at her horrified expression, then relented with, 'It's all right. I've had a word with them and they've found another room for you. Oh, by the way, we're only allowed one suitcase, so sort out what you really need and leave the rest in one of your cases here. The hotel will look after it until we come back at the end of the tour.'

Now he yawned, stretching his arms above his head. 'We'd better get to bed to be ready for the early start tomorrow.'

Etta shuddered. 'You said it's a six-thirty wake-up call?'

Kaan grinned almost maliciously.

'That's for the tourists. The staff — us — we get up at six. Just remember, you're not on holiday; you're here to work. Now go and repack your cases and then get some sleep.'

Etta's room was small and looked out on to a blank brick wall, not at all the kind of holiday accommodation she was used to. She got ready for bed in a very bad temper.

Brushing her smooth brown hair, she stared in the mirror at her pale oval face with its big hazel eyes. Normally any young man told that she was going to spend the next twelve days with him would have been scarcely able to believe his luck. Even if Kaan had been too preoccupied with the problems of the tour to take a good look at her, his reception had not been what she expected. He should have been full of gratitude, thanking her for the way she had taken Harry's place, not annoyed about her inexperience.

Etta sat down heavily on the edge of the bed, realising what a long and tiring day it had been. She should have been with her mother, about to start on a very comfortable holiday in the Mediterranean, so why was she here instead?

She recalled the fuss when Harry had fallen over and the consternation when it was realised how badly he had hurt himself, and the barely-hidden surprise with which the rest of the office had received her offer to replace Harry, because she was not known for offering to do extra work.

The truth was that she had acted on impulse. She had not been looking forward to two weeks with her mother, no matter how comfortable their surroundings, and coming to Turkey had seemed a way of avoiding her mother's company that would also bring her much-needed credit at work.

Remembering almost too late what Kaan had said about luggage, she hurriedly went through her cases, reluctantly abandoning many pretty but flimsy clothes in favour of the more practical garments she assumed she would need. Finally she climbed into bed and snuggled down, feeling suddenly lonely as she contemplated the days ahead in a strange land with an unfamiliar language — and in the company of a young man who had already shown his disapproval.

* * *

Determined not to give Kaan another excuse to complain, Etta had asked for a wake-up call at a quarter to six and stumbled downstairs, barely awake, half an hour after the insistent ringing of the phone had woken her from a very deep sleep. She found Kaan was already conferring with the hotel staff and he broke off to give her a curt nod and hand her a thick file of papers.

'You'll find coffee and some breakfast in the restaurant. Those papers give you a list of our passengers and where they come from. You can have a look through while you eat.'

She did manage a brief look after she had collected her coffee and croissant and it appeared that the thirty passengers had assembled from many different places. Some had flown in from Australia and New Zealand, there was a couple from Pakistan, one from Italy, and the remainder from Britain.

Kaan joined her. He was dressed all in black — jeans and a long-sleeved shirt open at the neck — and appeared far too alert and vigorous for such an early hour. Looking at him in the morning light, Etta saw that his eyes were golden, shaded by long lashes. With short, thick, dark hair and a healthy tan, she was forced to admit that he was undeniably good-looking.

It was a pity he was so unpleasant.

'You need to learn the names and who they belong to as quickly as possible,' he instructed her. 'People are happier when you address them by name. Now, this morning at the meeting I'll take a roll-call and you can tick them off on that list. Then I'll ask them their names when they get on the coach and you can tick them again. In fact, we check every time they get on and off the coach.'

'Doesn't that waste a lot of time? Is all that fuss really necessary?' she protested.

'Yes!' He scowled in reply. 'You'd be surprised how easily people go astray, and losing a passenger is every tour guide's nightmare.' He put down his coffee cup.

'Now, our driver is Ali. He's a good driver, very reliable, but he doesn't know much English and he's shy with women, so don't expect him to say much to you. He will have cleaned and tidied the coach by now and the porters should be bringing the luggage down. Let's make sure they're putting the cases in the right place,' he suggested. 'Give Reception the case you want them to keep for you.'

At least all the passengers found their way to the meeting. Etta watched them nervously as they filed in. She was going to be in constant close contact with them for several days. Would they be easy to get on with? Most of them were married couples, but there were also a few pairs of friends, and a few individuals who had come by themselves.

One man on his own, a man in his early forties with an easy, confident smile, caught Etta's eye. He nodded at her when he saw her watching him and his smile widened as if he liked what he saw and she found herself smiling back. At least she should have no problem with him.

Kaan greeted the tourists and rapidly explained the day-to-day procedure for the tour, answered a few questions, and promised to always be available if they needed help or information. At the end, when there were no more questions, he looked to where Etta was standing at the back of the room.

'If you can't find me,' he informed the group, 'then you can ask Etta — Etta Sanderson — my assistant.'

Thirty heads swivelled and thirty pairs of eyes looked at her appraisingly as she gulped and smiled weakly.

The meeting broke up and, as the tourists started to drift into little groups and chat to each other, a young woman approached Etta nervously.

'I'm Mary West,' she introduced herself, and lowered her voice conspiratorially as she looked round the room. 'It looks as if we are the only young ones in this lot of oldies, so we'll have to stick together.'

Etta didn't want anybody clinging to her while she was trying to learn her job. 'There's your husband; surely he'll be good company,' Etta pointed out, looking at the young man who had been sitting next to Mary West during the meeting and who was now asking Kaan some questions.

Mary blushed and giggled self-consciously. 'That's Gavin — Gavin Preston. He's not my husband yet. We're getting married next year, so this is a kind of pre-honeymoon.'

'Well, I'm sure you'll enjoy it,' responded Etta. Mary seemed eager to say more, but Etta seized the chance to move away as Kaan beckoned her.

'I've been looking at your outfit,' he announced.

Etta looked down at her denim jeans and white t-shirt. She had chosen them the night before after some deliberation, deciding the outfit would be comfortable as well as suitable for the climate.

'What's wrong with it? I thought it was very practical.'

'Oh, it is. But that's why hundreds of other women will be wearing exactly the same. You need to wear something that will stand out so that our clients can find you easily.'

He picked up a blazer from his chair and handed it to her. 'Put this on.'

Etta gazed at it in horror. It had broad orange, red and white stripes. Reluctantly she tried it on and found it was far too big for her. Impatiently she tore it off and handed it back to him, aware that he was trying — unsuccessfully — to conceal a smile that held a hint of mischief.

'I can't wear this! It makes me look awful!'

'True, it's not very becoming, but that doesn't matter. I know it's too big — that's because I got it for Harry — but it makes you stand out in a crowd and that's what matters, at least until our clients can recognise you easily.'

She glared at him and indicated his all-black outfit.

'And what about you? Will you be wearing one of these ghastly garments?'

He shook his head. 'For some reason they can always identify the man in black.' He held the blazer out to her. 'Now, come on or we'll be late.'

As he moved away with an easy, athletic grace, she saw how the eyes of many of the women followed him. It was true that it would be difficult to overlook him.

* * *

Now it was time for the passengers and their luggage to be put aboard the

18

coach, and at the last minute Etta remembered she hadn't left her extra case at Reception, so she snatched it back from the cases being loaded, hauled it in to the girl at the reception desk and gave a hurried explanation.

The coach finally drew away from the hotel soon after nine o'clock. Kaan gave a sigh of relief as he checked his watch and then relaxed in his seat beside Etta at the front of the coach.

'This is the restful bit,' he murmured. 'We can just sit back and leave it to the driver to get us to the next stop.'

Etta ignored him and sat fuming with the horrible blazer over her knees. She was already deeply regretting the impulse which had made her offer to come. She had survived other holidays with her mother, and she could probably have got on well enough with her this time. The two reps maintained their silence for a few minutes, and then Kaan turned to Etta.

'Well, we're going to spend the next few days together so we might as well get to know each other,' he said amicably enough. 'You told me you were all ready to go on holiday until you were asked to come here. Where were you going? Are you upset that you've ended up working here instead?'

Etta shook her head. Knowing she would be asked this, she had prepared an edited version of the truth.

'A relative was going somewhere and found she had room to take me along,' she told him. 'Actually, I wasn't looking forward to it much and I was quite glad to have an excuse not to go. This tour may be tough for me, but I really need to learn about what actually happens on the holidays we sell.' She looked at him. 'Can I ask you a question now?'

He nodded.

'Your name — Kaan Talbot — are you Turkish or British, or both?' she asked him.

'Both,' he replied. 'My father was English and my mother is Turkish and they met when he came to Turkey on holiday. We lived in England when I was a child but came here every year to see my Turkish relatives. My father died when I was sixteen, and when I left home to study tourism at university, my mother moved back to Turkey. I live in Turkey now, but I visit England and my relatives there quite often.'

'Which country do you prefer?'

'I like them both, although they are so different. Incidentally, Kaan means 'emperor',' he said with a wry grin. 'And while we're talking of names, where did Etta come from?'

'It's short for Henrietta, which I hate.'

'I see,' he mulled, then added, 'Any more questions?'

'Top Turkish Tours — I don't know much about them.'

'The firm is based in Istanbul and is very successful.'

'Who owns it?'

'It's a family-owned firm.'

He did not expand on this and the conversation lapsed. The smooth movement of the coach was lulling Etta to sleep after her early start and Kaan let her rest until a yawn informed him that she was stirring.

'We have a coffee stop soon,' he murmured. 'Culture and landscape are all very well, but you have to make sure there are enough toilet breaks.'

The comfort stop was a pleasant half-hour break at a café where she saw that some tourists were already buying small souvenirs. She wondered how heavy their cases would be by the end of the tour.

'And now it's on to Gallipoli,' Kaan said cheerfully as the bus took off again.

She looked at him vaguely. 'Where?'

He stared at her with incredulity and then a touch of anger. The temporary thaw in their relationship was clearly over.

'Gallipoli. Haven't you even read the itinerary?'

'I've glanced at it,' she said defensively, 'but I haven't had time to read it thoroughly, though I did bring a guide to Turkey with me. I was too busy last night sorting out my luggage — like you told me to.'

'Do you know anything about Gallipoli?'

'Nothing,' she was forced to admit. 'What is it?'

His lips were pressed together so tightly that they were almost white. 'Gallipoli,' he said at last, very carefully, 'was one of the most important episodes of the First World War.'

'The First World War?' she echoed. 'Well, I'm not surprised I've never heard of it. We didn't do modern history at school.'

'Have you heard of the Somme, of Ypres?'

She nodded reluctantly. 'They're always mentioned around Remembrance Day. They're somewhere in France, aren't they?'

'Oh, and because Gallipoli is in Turkey it isn't important, is that it? I suppose because the British lost, they prefer to forget the campaign!'

He turned away from her in disgust

and stared stonily ahead out of the window, leaving Etta feeling both guilty because of her ignorance and angry because he seemed to have expected her to master so much so soon.

Finally the coach drew up in a large car park and Kaan led the tourists to a green, tree-shaded cemetery near a beach where he gathered them into a group.

'Now, I know many of you know all about Gallipoli, but before we look round we might as well fill in any gaps in your knowledge.' He looked at Etta, standing on the edge of the group and obediently draped in the hideous blazer. 'Perhaps my assistant would like to give you a short talk on the subject?' Etta gazed helplessly at him, appalled, but he went on smoothly, 'On the other hand, it's one of my favourite sites, so I may know a bit more about it.'

For the next ten minutes he gave a clear account of the Gallipoli campaign, incorporating it into a survey of how significant it had been in Turkish history, and mentioning the role played in it by Ataturk, the great hero of modern Turkey.

Etta realised why the Australians and New Zealanders were so obviously fascinated by a campaign which had involved so many of their countrymen and could not help being impressed by Kaan's objectivity and the credit he gave to the soldiers of both sides. He held everyone's attention without trouble, his tall figure dominating the group.

After he had finished, the tourists were free to wander off and inspect the carefully tended cemeteries and the beach while Kaan made his way over to Etta.

'I hope you learned something about Gallipoli from my talk.'

'Yes. But I do know about ancient history,' she said defensively. 'I'm quite good on places like Troy.'

'Good. Then, as you are so knowledgeable, you can tell them all about it tomorrow morning, since that is where we are going. Or don't you feel quite ready for that yet?'

The challenge was completely unexpected, but her pride would not let her show him that she was instantly terrified at the prospect. 'All right. I can do it,' she claimed.

He gazed at her for a long second, and then nodded as though some unspoken question had been answered. 'Good. I look forward to hearing you.' He glanced round at the tourists, now widely spread throughout the site. 'Meanwhile, keep an eye on that couple who are wandering away. We don't want to lose them on the first day.'

'You sound like a shepherd looking after his flock.'

He laughed shortly. 'I tend to feel more like the sheepdog rounding them up.'

Etta wandered round the site, telling herself that she could already recognise Top Tour's clients among the other tourists now arriving in coach-loads. In one cemetery she found a man with his arm round his wife's shoulders as she wiped away her tears, but the woman shook her head when Etta asked if she could help, and pointed to one of the gravestones.

'This is my grandfather's grave,' she explained sadly. 'He was only twenty-two when he died, and my father was born two months later.'

Suddenly Etta could appreciate how important Gallipoli was to many of the tourists.

⋆   ⋆   ⋆

Back on the coach, every passenger counted aboard, they travelled on to the lunch stop — a pleasant, airy restaurant where two other coaches were already parked.

'We don't eat with the clients,' Kaan informed her as they made their way inside. 'It might inhibit their conversation, but we do stay in sight in case they want to speak to us.' He had a brief word with the restaurant owner, who shook Etta's hand vigorously when she was introduced, and then led her to a table where the two men who were escorting tourists in the other coaches were already seated. They looked at Etta with open interest and approval when Kaan introduced her to them.

'My new assistant, Etta Sanderson, who has bravely taken over at very short notice,' he informed them, before a waiter appeared to take their orders, instantly commanding everyone's full attention.

'Having a good season, Kaan?' one of the reps enquired midway through the meal.

'Reasonable,' Kaan responded. 'And you?'

The other man shrugged. 'Not bad.' He looked at Etta. 'And you get yet another pretty young lady as your assistant! You're a lucky man. What happened to the other one — the one with the funny name — Allegra?'

Etta saw Kaan's face suddenly set

hard. 'Nothing. She went back to Istanbul.'

His expression did not invite more questions.

★ ★ ★

By mid-afternoon the coach had reached the hotel where they would spend the night. A comparatively quiet first day gave the tourists a choice of going to bed early if they wanted to, or of taking the opportunity to spend time in the bar getting to know their travelling companions, and most chose the second option.

Already it was possible to see small groups forming, though Mary West seemed to make no effort to join in and stayed apart from the rest, even though her partner, Gavin, was chatting with some of the others.

The man who had caught Etta's eye at the welcome meeting met her walking out of the dining room. When they had name-checked everybody back

29

on the coach she had learned that his name was David Trowbridge.

Now he approached her and smiled invitingly. 'Let me buy you a drink. I'm here on my own,' he reminded her when he saw her surprised expression, 'and as one of the reps you're supposed to do all you can to keep me happy, which you'll do if you have a drink with me.'

She laughed at his obvious flattery, but agreed to the drink. After Kaan's disapproval it was pleasant to feel that someone had noticed her and found her attractive enough to want her company for a while.

'There aren't many solitary male travellers on this trip,' she remarked when they were seated.

'I had planned to come with a friend, a girlfriend.' David Trowbridge shrugged. 'But things didn't work out as I expected, so instead of giving up my holiday I'm here on my own. Fortunately it's easier to be a single traveller on a tour than on a beach holiday. I've been to plenty of

Turkish seaside resorts in the past few years so I thought I'd like to see a bit of the rest of the country.' He looked at her with obvious admiration. 'Now I'm glad I came.'

The compliment was good for her ego and Etta relaxed, enjoying his company. They chatted about the day, and Etta confessed that this was her first time in Turkey.

'If you want to know anything about the country and its customs you can ask me,' David Trowbridge offered, and then he shrugged. 'But I suppose you can get all the information you need from Kaan.'

'I'm sure I'll be glad of your help sometime,' she told him, an answer that seemed to satisfy him, for he asked her if she would like another drink, but before she could decide a middle-aged woman bustled up, interrupted their conversation unapologetically, and complained about her room.

'The air-conditioning doesn't work properly and it makes a lot of noise, and there isn't any soap in the bathroom.'

'Can't you tell Reception about that?' Etta asked her.

The woman's colour heightened noticeably.

'It's your job to sort out that kind of thing!'

Unsure what to do, Etta gave David Trowbridge an apologetic smile and reluctantly excused herself to go in search of Kaan, who she found in the hotel manager's office.

He groaned when she told him the problem.

'That must be Mrs Dankworth. She has already complained about her room last night, didn't like the restaurant where we had lunch, and says her seat is too cramped. Tomorrow it will be something else. There's always someone who likes making a fuss because it makes them feel important. I'll deal with her.'

Etta listened, impressed, as he greeted Mrs Dankworth sympathetically and asked how he could help. First he listened to the woman carefully for some minutes as she poured out her complaints, then he expressed his concern, and finally he promised immediate action. He then went back to the hotel manager, who telephoned a workman and assured Kaan that the minor problem with the noise would be rapidly solved and plenty of soap provided immediately. Kaan returned to the lady to give her the good news.

'Excellent!' she said. 'You, at least, are efficient.' She glared at Etta. 'Unlike some people who spend their time sitting doing nothing but drinking with any available man.'

She stalked away and Kaan turned to Etta, who was scarlet with rage and embarrassment.

'What was that about?'

'David Trowbridge asked me to have a drink with him and I accepted. What's the harm in that?' she enquired indignantly.

But Kaan was slowly shaking his head.

'Etta, that was a big mistake, especially so early in the tour. Your job is to be available to help all of the clients all of the time,' he explained. 'You mustn't even appear to favour one rather than another, let alone be seen to be possibly developing a friendship with one, or all the others will be watching to see if he gets any favours, such as a better room, and they'll make a big fuss if he does.'

He grimaced. 'I don't want to disappoint you, but there is always the possibility that he was in fact hoping to get preferential treatment from you. Also I should warn you that some travellers do seem to think that young women travel reps are fair game for a little holiday romance.'

'David Trowbridge just wanted someone to have a drink with,' she said hotly. 'I'm quite sure he was just being friendly.' She was tired, exhausted, and now she found herself blinking back tears. 'It's all right for you. You know all these things.'

Unexpectedly Kaan put an arm around her and smiled down at her sympathetically.

'Don't get upset. I wasn't always so well-informed. I made some terrible mistakes in the beginning. You'll soon learn, just as I did.' He grinned. 'When we've time, I'll tell you the full story of what happened when one woman summoned me to change a light bulb in her bedroom. When I got there, she was reclining on the bed wearing very little and obviously didn't need a light for what she was planning.'

Etta giggled. 'What did you do?'

'Some day, when you really need cheering up, I'll tell you. Meanwhile, I suggest you trot off to bed and get a good night's sleep. It's a very full day tomorrow — Troy and Izmir — and it's another early start, I'm afraid.'

Obediently she turned to leave, but his voice summoned her back. 'And remember, you're giving the talk about Troy.'

Etta went up to her room. In view of

her ignorance earlier that day, she spent some time reading her guide book and making notes, but at last she yawned, stretched and decided it was time for bed.

She had kept her shoulder bag with her on the coach, as it contained basic toiletries and various essentials from her passport to sun cream, but her clothes were all in her suitcase so she opened it in order to take out what she would wear the following morning. But when she flung the lid back she gasped and stared in horror as she found herself looking at the flimsy, impractical clothes she had intended to leave behind in Istanbul. She had snatched the wrong case from the coach!

All her essential clothes, such as her t-shirts, jeans and underwear, were now stored away in yesterday's hotel. Her first reaction was to imagine how stupid Kaan would think her, then desperately she scrabbled through the case's contents, hoping to find some wearable garments. She did find a very brief bra and pants set, but nothing else she could imagine wearing for the tour.

As the clock approached midnight she hastily rinsed out her t-shirt and hung it over the shower rail, hoping it would dry by morning. At last she switched the light off and nearly collapsed into bed, but instead of falling asleep instantly she found herself mentally rehearsing what she intended to say about Troy the following day.

Surprisingly, even when she had done that she found it difficult to sleep. She lay still, recalling what she had seen that day and the lessons she had learned, and she worried about the difficulties she might encounter in the future.

After a full day in his company, her feelings about Kaan were mixed. He had been cool, at first downright unpleasant, and then unexpectedly kind. One thing was clear, however. He was a very good travel rep and she could learn a lot from him.

As her heavy eyelids began to close at last, Etta decided she could understand why that unnamed woman had been so ready to welcome him to her bedroom. But there was still one thing she wanted to know — who was Allegra? And why had Kaan reacted so strongly to her name?

2

Etta's t-shirt hung limp and damp on the shower rail in the morning, obviously unwearable, and after desperately rifling through every garment in her suitcase she finally went down to breakfast wearing a flowered silk evening top that was not only completely unsuitable for daytime wear, but also clashed badly with her vividly striped blazer.

That was not her only problem. When she boarded the coach she hoped that Kaan could not hear the rustle of paper as she sat down. She had spent every available minute going over her preliminary notes for her introduction to Troy and had been busy writing down the most important bits of information about the ancient city in large letters, planning to hold them in her hand and sneak a look at them if necessary, and now there were several sheets of paper stuffed in her pocket.

'Ready for the day?' Kaan asked her, looking at her top with interest but making no comment.

'Just about,' she assured him, secretly crossing her fingers. She was not going to admit to him how scared she felt!

He glanced at her and seemed to hesitate before he spoke again. 'You don't have to give the introduction to Troy if you don't want to,' he said quietly. 'I was being rather mean, throwing you in at the deep end so soon.'

Etta's heart leapt. She could avoid the ordeal after all! But then, surprising herself, she decided she had to go through with it. She knew she was inclined to take the easy way out but she wasn't going to let Kaan think she couldn't cope. She just hoped she would not make a fool of herself in spite of all her efforts.

'Thank you,' she heard herself saying,

trying to sound calm, 'but I think I can manage.'

She felt him shrug, but he didn't say any more on the subject. Was he hurt because she had refused his kindness?

As the coach drove along she was bitterly regretting her pride. She was sure that if he offered once again to release her from giving the introductory speech she would accept instantly and she sat for several miles with her fists clenched, her nails biting into her palms, willing him to repeat his offer, but he stayed obstinately silent.

Some time later she realised that he was covertly inspecting what was visible of her blouse.

'That top will definitely make you easy to find,' he commented dryly when she sat up and pulled her blazer round her more tightly, 'but are you quite sure it is suitable? This is Troy in the morning, not some evening gala.'

'I left the wrong suitcase in Istanbul,' she confessed reluctantly. 'I did wash the t-shirt I wore yesterday but it didn't dry in time.'

'Well, I'm glad that gaudy rag wasn't your first choice,' he murmured disparagingly. 'At least it will give Mrs Dankworth something to criticise today — and if you'd worn yesterday's t-shirt she would have disapproved of you wearing that two days running anyway.'

His smile was reassuring and she felt much better when he told her that he was sure he had an answer to her problem. 'I'll phone the Istanbul hotel when we stop for lunch. There's a coach following this route which doesn't make as many calls as we do, and it should soon catch us up, so I'll ask the hotel to put your case on it.'

At first sight Troy was a disappointment — merely a series of hummocks with a few exposed crumbling stone walls and little to show that it was the site of one of the greatest stories in the world, except for an enormous wooden horse which dominated the entrance.

The tourists filed through the gate,

assembled dutifully in front of Kaan and Etta, and looked at them expectantly. Etta took a deep breath and stepped forward, sure everybody could see her hands trembling, acutely aware of how several women were eyeing the unbecoming combination of her hideous striped blazer and her blouse. She was miserably sure that some of her audience were even laughing at the spectacle she made. But she had voluntarily cut off her escape when she turned down Kaan's offer earlier, so she forced herself to smile, held her head high, cleared her throat, and began her carefully prepared speech, avoiding eye-contact with the tourists.

Gripping her notes tightly in one hand, she started by pointing out that Homer's Troy had only been one of a series of cities on the same site and that gradual silting up meant the sea was now much further away than it had been in Troy's glory days so long ago. She knew her voice sounded shrill and that although the audience was listening dutifully its members were obviously not gripped by the information she was providing.

Suddenly Etta felt impatience boiling up within her. She would not have been very interested in these dry facts herself, so why should her listeners be? She tucked her notes in her pocket and looked straight at her audience.

'Some people say that the Trojan wars were really trade wars, and if you are interested in that kind of history you can ask me later, but, as often happens, the myth is more important than the actual history. What really interests people,' Etta declared, 'is the story of Helen of Troy, the most beautiful woman in the world, and her lover, Paris. People want to learn about Hector and Achilles and the other heroes of the Trojan war that lasted for ten long years and ended with the fall of Troy.' It was a story that had always fascinated her and now she went on to tell the ancient tale of a love that had destroyed a city and killed thousands.

As she recounted the story she relaxed, forgetting that she was speaking to a group of virtual strangers, forgetting her strangely-dressed appearance, and her voice reflected her feelings about heroes such as Hector and his opponent, Achilles. The tourists listened attentively, her emotion affecting them. When she stopped speaking she was surprised by a spontaneous round of applause. For her? But there were smiles and congratulations as well.

'A storyteller to rival Homer himself!' declared Kaan, who had joined in the applause. 'Now, if you'll follow me I'll show you some points of interest. One archaeologist found a hoard of gold at Troy. He claimed it was jewellery that had belonged to Helen of Troy. With a bit of luck we might find another treasure hoard — in which case, I want half!'

Etta closed her eyes briefly, rejoicing that the ordeal was over, and dutifully followed him together with the rest, glad that her talk had been well received but with reaction making her feel a little shaky.

She found David Trowbridge beside her, smiling congratulations. 'Well done! I enjoyed that, and I learned quite a bit. You are really quite a scholar.'

She smiled up at him gratefully, reassured by his comments, then saw that Mrs Dankworth was watching them carefully, so she discreetly moved away.

Mary West was the next to approach her.

'It is a marvellous story,' she said shyly, then suddenly frowned and darted a black look at her partner, Gavin Preston, who was deep in conversation with another member of the party. 'Isn't it a pity that in real life, some people have absolutely no idea of romance?'

Oh, dear! It sounded as though there had been a lover's tiff! Well, she would not get involved. Mary would have to find someone else to confide in.

Perhaps some mature lady, with the experience of years of matrimony, could give Mary some good advice.

'Well, in the end romance didn't do Helen or Paris much good,' she observed, and then turned to respond to another woman who wanted some historical point explained.

Later she saw Gavin trying to draw Mary into his conversation, but the girl turned away. Etta thought that was a mistake. If Mary got to know the other tourists, it might compensate for Gavin's apparent lack of romance.

Back on the coach, Kaan made it clear that his congratulations had been sincere. 'Not bad for a first attempt. Of course, you were lucky. There aren't a great many solid facts known about Troy, so you didn't have to learn a lot and could rely on the story. Still, you definitely kept everybody interested.'

'Nearly everybody,' she corrected him. 'There are two men who came together — Burke and Hunt — they looked bored the whole time.'

'I noticed that. They were the same yesterday at Gallipoli.' Kaan frowned. 'Sometimes I wonder why people come on a tour like this if they aren't interested in the history, ancient or modern. Some just don't seem to check the details in the brochure before they book. Perhaps they expected Turkey to be one long round of belly dancers. Still, so long as they behave themselves we don't have to worry about them.'

She settled back in her seat, absurdly happy with her success, and particularly pleased that even Kaan thought she had done well. Even her clashing blouse and blazer no longer seemed to matter.

The rest of the day was spent driving through beautiful countryside, never far from the sea, with a brief stop in a modern port which seemed a world away from the ancient battles of Troy.

There Etta found a street market where eager stallholders tried to sell her t-shirts printed with various slogans and pictures, some verging on the pornographic. She rejected them all and managed to find a plain white t-shirt which she hurriedly put on in a handy toilet, abandoning the very expensive silk top and hoping its finder would appreciate it.

Then the coach drove on until they reached their destination for the night in a popular seaside resort, Kusadasi.

Once again dinner was served fairly early, this time so that those who wanted to could explore the evening pleasures of the resort. Etta was wondering what to do with herself, or what she was expected to do, when Kaan approached her.

'Would you like to come for a stroll along the seafront with me? We can have a drink somewhere. It's one of our few chances to take a break away from the clients during the tour.'

The invitation seemed to mark his growing approval and acceptance of her and she accepted readily before hurrying up to her room to change. Another silk top would not be out of place this evening. Kaan did not comment when she returned, but his eyes showed his approval.

'Let me show you Kusadasi — and I think Kusadasi will be delighted to see you.'

She took his arm and they turned towards the exit, but just as they reached the reception area the hotel's front door was flung open and a woman swept in imperiously. She was tall, elegant, and beautifully dressed in clothes that were apparently simple but obviously expensive. She was mature but in no way showing any unwelcome signs of age. Her dark hair had been arranged by a skilled professional and those she passed experienced the hint of a very expensive perfume. Etta stopped dead at the sight of her and turned pale.

'Oh, no! Not now!' she exclaimed faintly. She dropped Kaan's arm and tried in vain to hide behind a pillar, but the woman had already seen her and her eyes narrowed purposefully as she changed direction and strode towards Etta.

'Henrietta! Your employers told me you would be here.'

Kaan stepped forward and coughed politely. 'Can I help?'

He was ignored.

'I told them they had no right to ruin our arrangements.' The woman looked round the lobby and shuddered with distaste. 'I'll wait while you collect your things then you can come with me.'

Kaan's voice hardened as he refused to be ignored any longer. 'Madam, Miss Sanderson is my assistant,' he told her firmly. 'If you are trying to interfere with her duties, you will have to discuss it with me.'

Indignant colour rose in the woman's face as she turned, preparing to confront him, but Etta intervened quickly.

'It's all right, Kaan. This is — this is my mother, and I'll deal with the situation.' She turned to the newcomer.

51

'Now, Mother . . . ' she began, but got no further.

'Henrietta, what you're doing is ridiculous! You were supposed to be coming on holiday with me straight from that ghastly London office. Your firm had no right to send you trailing round with a busload of tourists and you shouldn't have allowed yourself to be bullied into it. The yacht is at Izmir until tomorrow, so you can leave with me now and spend the next couple of weeks cruising the Mediterranean, just as we planned.'

Etta, horrified, saw that some of the tourists were looking their way, attracted by the raised voices. One or two, including Mrs Dankworth, were beginning to drift, accidentally on purpose, in her direction.

'Please, Mother, come with me and we'll talk it over,' she said urgently, and hurried away into the almost deserted lounge so that the newcomer was forced to follow, high heels clicking impatiently on the tiled floor. Etta indicated a quiet corner where they could sit down without being over-heard. Her mother inspected the seat first as if expecting it to be too dirty to receive her, then deigned to sit while Etta hurried to say what she wanted before her mother could issue any more commands.

'Mother, I wasn't forced to come here. I offered, because it was an opportunity to get invaluable experience which will help with my job.' Mentally she added, *And to avoid being ordered about by you for two weeks.*

She pushed her fingers wearily through her hair and stared stubbornly at her furious parent. 'Look, remember when you told me that I should get a job and find out how the real world worked? Well, now I have a job, and I like it and I intend to go on doing it, and I'm sorry if it upsets the holiday arrangements you had planned for me. I enjoy what I'm doing on this tour, and I find holidaying on the yacht boring, so I'm staying here.'

Her mother shook her head impatiently. 'Oh, do grow up!' she snapped. 'I know I told you to get a job, but it was because I was annoyed with you, and since then you have tried a few things. But I didn't mean that you should get a *permanent* job. There's no need for that, as you well know. You don't have to work five days a week for someone else so you can earn enough to live on. I've done that, dear, and it's a miserable life. You don't have to suffer as I did.'

'I want to prove that I can be independent — if I want to be.'

Her mother blinked incredulously. 'Independence? What's the point of that? People want money — freedom from worry, that's real independence — and I can give you that.'

'I don't want to always be given things! I want to prove that I can earn them for myself, that I deserve them!'

Her mother clicked her tongue and looked at her small gold watch. 'There's obviously no point in talking to you now when you're in this mood, and I promised George I'd be back by nine.' She sighed. 'Now, listen to me. If I leave you to think things over, I suppose it's possible you might come to your senses, especially after another day dragging tourists around. After all, you have come running back to me before when you've got tired of those other jobs,' she went on, brightening. 'I'll tell the chauffeur to bring the car here tomorrow evening and it will be waiting for you at seven o'clock precisely. The yacht sails tomorrow evening, so if he comes back without you, you will have missed your last chance to get away from this.'

Her face softened and she stretched out a hand to Etta. 'I can give you everything you could possibly want, Henrietta, and that's what I want to do — to make you safe and happy.' She forced a laugh. 'And it will only be the three of us on the yacht. I have learned from past experience and I promise you I haven't got any eligible young men hidden in the cabins.'

Etta managed a smile and took her mother's hand.

'I know you want the best for me, Mother, and I am grateful. It's just that we seem to have different ideas about what will make me happy.'

Her mother was about to speak again, but Etta hushed her. 'I promise I will think it over.' She smiled mischievously. 'But now I think I'd better tell my boss that I'm not deserting him without warning tonight. That would have caused problems.'

'Do you mean you have to take orders from that impertinent young man who kept interfering?'

'He doesn't order me about, he tells me what I am supposed to do, and I'm learning a lot from him.'

Her mother gave her a disbelieving look before the two women rose and Etta saw her mother out to where a chauffeur-driven limousine was occupying an inordinate amount of space in front of the hotel. They kissed and parted, and as the car drove away Etta turned back in search of Kaan, only to see him standing by the door, having watched the little scene with obvious fascination.

He lifted an eyebrow in curiosity as she approached. 'You're staying, then?'

'Evidently — though my mother clearly thinks I'm mad.'

'In that case, do you still want that coffee?'

Etta nodded gratefully and let him guide her to a small café five minutes from the hotel. There she leaned back in her chair and closed her eyes, breathing deeply until she heard the chink of the coffee cups.

When she looked up, she saw Kaan watching her.

'I suppose you'll want to know what that was all about,' she said wearily.

'Of course,' he replied. 'In fact, if you don't tell me, I won't be able to sleep. Then the coach will be hours late setting off and the tour will be ruined.'

She was reluctantly forced to laugh,

and then took a sip of coffee. 'Well, as you will have gathered, that was my mother.'

'I also gathered that you gave up the chance of cruising the Mediterranean in a yacht in order to help steer our clients around Turkey. Not many girls would have done that.'

'I had the choice and I chose to stay here,' she said flatly. 'I suppose you won't understand that without knowing a bit more about my background, especially my mother.' She took a deep breath and sipped her coffee again while Kaan waited patiently to hear her story.

'My parents met when they were very young.' She hesitated, frowning. 'I don't really know much about my father, except that he was charming but irresponsible. I was a mistake — my mother has often told me that — and when she informed him that she was going to have a baby he accused her of trying to trap him and disappeared soon afterwards. So my mother was left

58

alone with me. She had virtually no support from her family, who blamed her for the situation and thought she should have had me adopted.

'She got a job in an office where she earned just enough to park me in a nursery for the day, pay for a roof over our heads, and feed us, though I was so young at the time that I can't remember much about that. After a while she married her boss and helped build the firm up. Then she met an even richer businessman, so she got a divorce and married him.

'She's on her fourth husband now and will never have to worry about money again.'

'And she is obviously willing to share her good fortune with you. So why are you working in a travel firm, getting up at the crack of dawn and dealing with people like Mrs Dankworth?'

Etta shrugged while wondering how she could explain to him without revealing too much of her inner self, and then proceeded to give him a brief summary of the facts, aware that she wished she could present herself in a better light than her story showed.

'During my teens I was tucked away in a boarding school where I found I had a brain and worked hard enough to pass a few exams. My teachers said I could have a good career if I tried, but I had no idea what I really wanted to do with my life, no burning ambition. So after I left school I admit it was easier to just drift into enjoying a life of luxury living with my mother.

'Then one day we had an awful row because I was complaining that I couldn't have some expensive piece of unnecessary junk. Looking back, it showed just how spoilt I was, and how ungrateful. My mother lost her temper and told me I should get a job and find out how the rest of the world lived.

'The next morning I woke up feeling rather ashamed of myself. I thought about what she'd said, and realised that I didn't want to spend my life trailing after my mother like an unwanted piece of baggage.' She looked urgently at Kaan. 'That's not the right thing to say! I'm not unwanted, and I know my mother really cares for me, but she's better at giving orders than showing affection. Anyway, I spent that day really thinking. It made me finally decide that I should learn to be a person in my own right and develop my own talents — if I had any.'

She shook her head sadly. 'The only trouble was that I didn't seem to have any special talents. I tried a few jobs before I joined the travel agency, but I always got bored or thought I was expected to do too much, and instead of persevering it was always easier to give the job up and go home to Mother. But I do like the travel agency — and I would like to stay there and make a go of it.'

'Is your mother's current husband willing to have you around?'

'George? Oh, yes. In fact I quite like him — and he seems to like having me with them. He's older than Mother, so he's sold his business, is very rich, and loves boats.'

'But you don't?'

'I don't mind them for a few days, but then sunbathing and swimming to fill in the time get boring.' She fidgeted. 'And you can bet that if there are guests on board — then one of them will be some young man that Mother considers would be a suitable husband for me. The only trouble is that I never fancy them and they always seem more eager to please my mother and George than please me.'

She frowned. 'My mother is an attractive woman and, as you will have realised, a very strong personality. I always feel plain and colourless beside her.'

Kaan bent his head so she could not see his face but she knew from the way his shoulder shook that he was laughing. She looked at him indignantly.

'My dear Miss Henrietta Sanderson,' he said with mock solemnity, 'you are far from colourless, and nobody could ever call you plain.'

Before she could digest this remark he stood up.

'Well,' he said, 'as you've apparently decided you'd rather stay with the tour and keep Mrs Dankworth happy than cruise round the Mediterranean in luxury, we'd better get some sleep. It's another busy day tomorrow.' He gave her a straight look. 'You may be Little Miss Rich Girl, but while you're with this tour you have to work hard, and I'll see you do.'

'I realise that! You've made it quite clear what you expect of me,' she said indignantly. 'And anyway we can't go yet. I think you owe me something. I've told you my story. Now I want to know about Allegra. I saw how you reacted when her name was mentioned, and I've been wondering about her ever since.'

His lips tightened and for a moment she thought he would refuse to answer, but then he looked at her with

63

resignation and sat down again.

'I suppose I can tell you. It's a short, stupid story, anyway, and it doesn't show me in a very good light.

'Allegra, like you, was sent on one trip with me to learn the business. She was very beautiful, we spent the days together, and of course I fell for her. I must say in my own defence that she led me on and flirted with me outrageously.

'On the last day of the tour we said goodbye to the clients but the two of us were staying on in the hotel that night. That evening I knocked at her room door with a bottle of wine in one hand and two glasses in the other, sure that we were going to spend a very happy night together.'

He stopped and grimaced. 'She laughed at me, admitted she'd been encouraging me, but said she was just doing it for fun, and then she shut the door in my face. I took the wine back to my room and drowned my sorrows and the next day she behaved as though nothing had happened, waved goodbye to me, and I've never seen her again.'

Etta gazed at him with mixed feelings. Kaan's behaviour had been stupid, but such an attractive man could not have received many such refusals, and Allegra's rejection must have bruised his ego badly.

'Had you really fallen for her?'

He gave a short laugh and shook his head. 'Fortunately, no. But I behaved like an immature idiot and my pride was badly hurt and she made me feel a fool. I've got over it, though I must say in my defence that she was one of the most beautiful girls I've ever seen. Smooth, blonde, shining hair and brown eyes, and a perfect skin!'

Etta was suddenly conscious of how the day's sun had reddened her nose. She looked at Kaan's face and wondered if he had indeed completely recovered from the rejection.

On the way back to the hotel, he asked her what had happened to her father. 'Have you ever met him? Does he have any contact with you at all?'

'I've never seen him or heard from him and I wouldn't recognise him if I met him. I don't know what happened to him after he left my mother. She may know something, but if so she's never told me. He just vanished. But I've got one souvenir of him. He was called Harry — Henry — so that's why I got landed with Henrietta.'

Back at the hotel, Kaan nodded and smiled to a couple from their tour who were just coming back from the town.

'At least they'll be in a fit state for sightseeing tomorrow,' he commented to Etta. 'There are always a few who drink too much, wake up with hangovers, and either miss the sights or drag round miserably dosing themselves with aspirin. Anyway, we're here for two nights, so at least they won't have to pack.'

Two more figures appeared — the two men who were travelling together and who so far seemed to have been bored by everything they'd seen.

Kaan's eyes narrowed. 'Mr John Burke and Mr Geoff Hunt.' The strap of a grey shoulder bag with navy-blue piping was slung across Geoff Hunt's chest. 'He never seems to move anywhere without that bag. He keeps hold of it on the coach and I noticed he even kept it slung across him during lunch.'

'Maybe he's had things stolen from him at some time, so now he's extra careful,' Etta suggested.

'Possibly, and I suppose if he's willing to put up with the discomfort it doesn't matter to us. However, I'd still like to know why the two of them came on this tour. Perhaps I'll get a chance to talk to them tomorrow.' He yawned. 'It's off to Ephesus in the morning — one of our most important visits and one of the most tiring — so get a good night's sleep and a good breakfast.'

They separated and Etta went up to her room.

Once again, unlike the guests who all had sea views, she had a room which looked out into a dark central well. It was adequate, but that was really all you could say in its favour.

Etta was guiltily aware that she hadn't told Kaan she would still have one more chance to escape the tour tomorrow evening when her mother's limousine would be waiting to carry her away. As she moved round the poky little room she grew a little wistful at the thought of her stepfather's luxurious yacht and the large cabin she would have occupied.

As she washed her bra and pants in the bathroom basin and hung them over the shower rail, she remembered that on the yacht all her laundry would of course have been done for her, and that there were servants there who would have tidied up after her and waited for her to announce her slightest wish so they could rush to satisfy it.

She remembered the quarrel with her mother that she had told Kaan about, the one which had first persuaded her to get a job. She had complained to her mother that her allowance wasn't enough and that she needed more money. She had obviously caught her mother at a bad time, for instead of automatically increasing her allowance her mother had rounded on her and called her a spoilt brat.

She sighed. Her mother had been right, but when it came to it Etta knew she really didn't have to prove herself to anyone except her mother and herself. Was she being foolish, traipsing round the country with a coachload of strangers? In a few days they would fly home and she would never see them again. They would soon forget whatever she did for them. As her mother had pointed out that evening, money had its advantages.

She began to unbutton her blouse, but was interrupted by the bedside telephone ringing. She was tempted to ignore it, feeling that her working day was done, but then reluctantly picked it up. It was the hotel receptionist urgently asking Miss Sanderson to come down straight away as there was a problem with one of her clients. Etta could hear raised voices over the phone, so hastily she redid her buttons and made for the lift.

At the reception desk she found a New Zealand couple from the tour in heated discussion with a man who was apparently the taxi driver who had brought them back from a bar in the resort in town.

'We're not paying him that amount!' declared the husband. 'It's far too much for the distance we came. It's robbery!'

The taxi driver was demanding that Etta come and look at his meter. Everybody was speaking at the same time, and nobody would listen when she tried to calm them down.

Then Kaan appeared. His incisive voice cut through the hubbub and silenced them all for a vital few seconds. When the taxi driver pressed forward, eager to get his complaint in first, and the husband began to protest loudly, Kaan insisted that the driver and his passengers should each give their side of the story in turn without interruption.

He listened to both and then spoke to the driver rapidly in Turkish. Before the New Zealanders could object he turned to them. In a surprisingly short time money was handed over and matters were settled, apparently to everyone's satisfaction.

'I didn't follow that,' Etta confessed as the driver tucked the notes into his pocket and left the hotel while the couple made for the lift. 'Who was at fault?'

'Both sides, in a way,' Kaan said wearily. 'Our clients had got the exchange rate wrong, so the driver wasn't asking as much as they thought, but he had brought them home a long way round so I insisted he reduce his bill a bit.' He shrugged. 'Most problems end up being solved by compromise and common sense. I'm sorry the receptionist had to disturb you. She didn't realise I was outside, talking to someone.'

'It was no trouble. After all, I'm here to deal with problems so I didn't panic.'

Kaan smiled down at her. 'Really? Do you know that your top two buttons are in the wrong holes, leaving a somewhat interesting view?'

Etta's fingers flew to her blouse fastening and she reddened, said goodnight rather stiffly and left for her room.

Once there, she suddenly felt extremely tired. It had been another long day, complicated by her mother's unexpected appearance. She barely had the energy to undress and pull her nightdress over her head before she fell on the bed, pulled up the covers and fell fast asleep.

There was certainly no time to debate further whether she should choose to continue the coach tour or be ready tomorrow evening to let the chauffeur drive her to the yacht.

3

In marked contrast to Troy, much of the ancient city of Ephesus had survived, and in places the façades of classical ruins lining the roads made it possible to imagine for a few, fleeting moments that you were in the bustling city of two thousand years ago when Saint Paul was preaching there.

As a result, just like the city in its prime, modern Ephesus was big and noisy, and very, very busy — full of passengers from several cruise ships who had docked at a nearby port and been bussed to the site for their daily dose of culture.

After Kaan had managed to find a comparatively quiet spot and given his charges a brief general introduction, he urged them to go and explore by themselves.

'As you can see, the place is too full

for us to go round as a group. You wouldn't be able to hear me speak, for one thing,' he pointed out. 'Just remember where the exit is and be back . . . ' He stopped and peered at his watch. 'Let's say we'll meet at the gate in an hour and a half. Enjoy yourselves.'

Mrs Dankworth objected immediately. 'I want to be told about things. How will I know what's important and what isn't?'

'Everywhere else we can escort you round, but I'm afraid Ephesus is a special case. It's just too popular,' Kaan said patiently, waving his arm at the crowds. 'I can assure you that there is adequate information at various points — and Miss Sanderson and I will be walking round, so you can ask us questions when you see us.'

The group split up, though Mrs Dankworth was muttering darkly to another woman, a Miss Pritchard, with whom she had become friendly. Finally everyone had wandered slowly off in various directions.

Etta waited for Kaan to give her instructions. 'What do we do?' she asked.

'What I said. We wander off as well, very slowly, towards the most popular areas. Sooner or later some of our group will be looking for us because they will want questions answered. Some will be about the history of Ephesus, but others will be asking if they can get a cup of coffee or where the toilets are.'

'Oh! So I can just walk round with you?'

'No,' he said firmly. 'We split up. Then they'll be twice as likely to find one of us.'

Of course he was right. Five minutes after Etta had reluctantly left him to follow one of the main paths, one client seized her by the arm and wanted a detailed explanation of the various types of Greek column. Fortunately she managed to find the answer in her guide book.

After that, two wanted coffee and she

was able to direct them to the cafe. But gradually, half on purpose, Etta found herself drifting away to the less frequented areas of the ancient city. She felt a little guilty, but it was very peaceful and soothing to be able to wander around by herself and appreciate the surviving antiquities without being pestered by clients.

As the sun grew hotter she slipped off the horrible blazer and draped it over her arm, inside out, aware that this would make it difficult for members of the tour to pick her out. Let the tourists look after themselves for once.

She eventually found herself near the area which, two thousand years ago, had been the old marketplace. It was one of the less obviously appealing areas, an empty square surrounded by the sad remains of colonnades, and it was virtually deserted. Etta was delighting in her rare moment of solitude until she realised with some annoyance that even there she could not escape members of her party.

John Burke and Geoff Hunt were visible, Hunt distinguished as always by the shoulder bag slung across his shoulder. Etta supposed the two men might be lost, or just ignorant of where the more interesting sights were. She sighed resignedly and dutifully began to make her way towards them but then stopped before they became aware of her presence. The two were in the shadow of a ruined building, but she had seen movement and realised that they were already talking to someone. Craning her neck, she caught a glimpse of that person and realised with surprise that it was David Trowbridge.

Well, he could probably help them if they needed it. Then yet another figure appeared from the shadows and joined the little group — a man she did not recognise.

The four were deep in discussion so quietly she crept away, wondering who the stranger was. Maybe it was an expert who was fascinating them with his knowledge of the city — though he would have a hard job inspiring Burke and Hunt.

Soon she was back among the crowds and, looking at her watch, she realised with a shock that it was nearly time for the group to get back to the coach. She should be there to greet them and count them on, but in her haste she took a couple of wrong turnings and was one of the last to arrive at the gate, receiving a sharp look from Kaan, who was already surrounded by a dozen tourists.

'The coach is just over there,' he pointed out. 'So let's get on it. I'm sure you all feel like a rest and then lunch after fighting your way round Ephesus.'

He handed Etta the list of tourists. 'Check them on,' he instructed. 'And put your blazer back on so that everybody can see you by the coach. I'll just go back a short way and see if there are any stragglers I can round up.'

The tourists were indeed ready for a rest and several of them, hurrying ahead of Etta, were already on the coach before she could start ticking the names off. Flustered, she started a roll call but it was complicated by the arrival of half-a-dozen latecomers.

Kaan appeared. 'Is everybody here?' he asked her.

She stared down the body of the coach. There were a few empty seats, but the coach hadn't been full to start with, and she was reluctant to admit her failure to check properly.

'Well?' Kaan said impatiently.

'I think so,' she said, unwillingly. 'Yes, they are all here.'

He sat down and nodded to the driver to start, but just as the coach began to move there was an urgent shout from one of the back seats.

'Stop! We've left two behind! They're just coming!'

Kaan spoke urgently to the driver and the coach stopped abruptly. The New Zealand couple, who'd had the confrontation with the taxi driver the other night, came puffing up and almost fell into the coach as the driver opened the door.

'You weren't going to leave us, were you?' they asked unbelievingly as they clambered along the aisle to their seats.

'Of course not,' said Kaan smoothly. 'We were just getting nearer the exit so you would find us more easily.'

Etta closed her eyes in shame as he sat down again and waited for his reaction to her carelessness. She could feel the tension but he didn't speak to her or look at her and maintained his silence until they reached the restaurant where they were to have lunch. Etta was left to spend the intervening time imagining what would have happened if the couple had arrived a few seconds later, and knew she deserved all that Kaan might say to her. She waited till all the clients had filed into the restaurant and then turned to him.

'I got flustered. I'm sorry,' she said miserably.

'So you should be,' he said with icy fury. 'I thought I'd got it through to you that you have to make sure that nobody gets lost. It's better to keep the coach waiting, to check again and again, rather than risk abandoning people in a strange country. You were unforgivably careless.'

'I feel dreadful,' she said weakly. 'What could they have done if they'd found the coach had gone when they got here?'

'Neither of them speak Turkish. They would have been panicking, wondering what on earth to do. I suppose with luck they could have got a taxi to chase after us — or phoned our head office if they had the number with them and a mobile phone. Then we would have been in real trouble!'

* * *

Lunch, once again separated from the tourists, passed mostly in silence. Towards the end Etta mentioned tentatively that she had seen Burke and Hunt, together with David Trowbridge and a stranger.

'I still don't know what they're doing on this tour,' she brooded, but Kaan did not seem interested.

'Maybe they're just enjoying a break from their families, maybe they have some common interest in Turkey that we'll find out later. Maybe getting away from something in England is more important than being in Turkey. People come on holiday for all sorts of reasons. Maybe they just want to be together. And stop blushing! Are you shocked by the young unmarried couple — Mary West and Gavin Preston?'

'Of course not.' Her voice softened. 'They are very young; both in their early twenties.'

'Young and romantic, like Romeo and Juliet, and just as inexperienced. I hope all goes smoothly for them, because I'm not sure how well they'd cope with any problems, and we don't want one unhappy couple spoiling the atmosphere for the rest.'

'Well, at least we won't be expected

to help with their personal relationship, will we?'

'You'd be surprised how often people have expected me to act as agony aunt! We tell them we're here to help in any way we can, and they do take us literally.

'Now I suggest you stop worrying about our clients' personal affairs, which are nothing to do with us, and concentrate on making sure we don't lose any of them.'

After lunch, keenly aware of Kaan watching her, Etta counted the passengers back on the coach very carefully indeed. David Trowbridge, almost the last on, lingered for a few words.

'You are proving a very capable nursemaid,' he laughed, indicating her list.

'I'm doing my best.'

At that moment she saw Burke and Hunt emerge from the restaurant and nodded towards them.

'Aren't they an odd couple!' she commented and waited for his reaction.

Trowbridge glanced towards them casually. 'I wouldn't know. I haven't spoken to them yet,' he murmured, and moved up into the coach, leaving Etta rather taken aback.

Why he was lying to her? Then another couple of passengers arrived and she forgot about him.

Kaan had nodded his guarded approval of her careful name-checking, and as they set off once again his tone became almost sympathetic. 'As you realised, I was angry with you this morning, but that was because I know what can happen in such a situation. When I'd just started in travel I was touring with a more experienced rep. I was supposed to be learning from him, but he had got a little careless. After one excursion someone pointed out that a couple was missing a few minutes after the coach had actually set off, so we drove back at full speed to pick them up.

'They were furious with us, even threatened to sue us for abandoning them, and for the rest of the tour they took every opportunity to criticise us or make unpleasant remarks. Another tourist got fed up with them and told them it was their own fault for being late. The rest took sides, and the whole tour was spoilt.

'At least, I can tell you if you do it once you are very unlikely to ever do it again. So I hope you've learned your lesson.'

★ ★ ★

It took them longer than expected to return to Kusadasi. As the coach approached the town it was caught up in a great queue of traffic that seemed to stretch for miles. Police cars sped noisily along the hard shoulder.

'Has there been an accident? Can you see?' someone asked, peering ahead.

Kaan unfastened his seat belt and stood up. 'I'll just try and find out what's happening while none of the cars are moving,' he told the passengers.

They saw him moving along the road, bending to speak to the car drivers. Ten minutes later, when he returned, the coach hadn't moved an inch and everybody looked at him expectantly as he climbed back in.

'At least it's not an accident,' he announced. 'Apparently there was a big robbery in Kusadasi last night. A jeweller's shop was broken into and two men were badly injured when they disturbed the robbers. The police are searching cars and questioning people — that's what's causing the gridlock. We can't do anything to hurry things up so I suggest you just relax and wait patiently.'

The coach grew hot and stuffy and everyone heaved a sigh of relief when, forty minutes later, the long lines of cars and lorries ahead of them began to move slowly and gradually the coach crept onwards until, an hour late, they reached their hotel.

Etta was relieved when she was able to go to her own room. Ephesus had been hot and dusty and the long wait on the coach had been an endurance test. Gratefully she stripped off her clothes, dropped them on the floor, and had a long shower.

She emerged reluctantly, towelled herself roughly and then, lacking the energy to dress again immediately, sank down on the bed. Ephesus had been physically exhausting and she had not found it particularly interesting because she had been too busy answering questions to appreciate it.

Then she had nearly been responsible for abandoning the two tourists and Kaan had been justifiably furious with her, then finally there had been the long crawl back to the hotel. She looked miserably round the small room, at the bare furnishings and the pile of discarded clothes which she would have to tidy up. She'd had enough! She wanted to escape from this tour.

Then, suddenly, she remembered

that she could! At seven o'clock she could walk out of the hotel, climb into the waiting limousine to be driven off to her stepfather's yacht, and she could forget all about nagging women like Mrs Dankworth and idiots who couldn't find a coach in time, and she would never see Kaan again. That last thought made her hesitate. She was aware that Kaan's approval was becoming very important to her, and she could imagine the contempt he would inevitably feel for her if she took the easy way out and deserted the tour.

But in a few days' time the tour would end and then she and Kaan would part anyway — so his good or bad opinion of her wouldn't matter whatever she did.

She found her watch. It was six o'clock. The limousine would be here in an hour. Suddenly full of renewed energy, she scrambled off the bed, dressed hurriedly, and began to thrust the few belongings which she had unpacked into her shoulder bag. She would take her suitcase with her, of course. The pretty clothes it contained would be wanted on the yacht.

When she'd finished, Etta took a final look round her room. Well, she wouldn't have to put up with such a miserable room any more! All she needed now was a porter to bring her suitcase down. But she couldn't be a complete coward and just vanish. First she had to tell Kaan what she was going to do.

Taking a deep breath, she opened the door and prepared to go downstairs to face him, her heart thumping as she thought of his reaction. But before she had walked more than a few yards, one of the doors opened and an anxious woman eagerly seized her arm.

'Miss Sanderson, I don't know what to do! The bracket holding the shower head fell off the wall when I went to use it. Honestly, I didn't pull it off.'

'Don't worry, Miss Owens. It was probably coming loose. I'll get the hotel to send a workman to fix it.'

She inspected the damage and, with Miss Owens standing nervously by, she called Reception, who promised to send a workman up immediately. Miss Owens was almost tearfully grateful. Etta knew that it was the elderly woman's first trip abroad, had seen how she was delighting in the adventure, and was glad that she had been able to solve the problem for her.

It gave her a warm glow of self-satisfaction — which vanished when she reached the ground floor and saw Kaan with some of the clients. As heads turned towards her, he became aware of her presence and came to greet her with a smile.

'Good news! Istanbul managed to put your suitcase on a lorry which was coming to Kusadasi. It's at Reception and I've asked them to send it up to your room.'

She hesitated. How could she tell him that the suitcase could stay where it was because she was leaving? Suddenly it was impossible to tell him face to face that she was taking the easy way out yet again, and once more giving up when things got difficult. Instead, she found herself thanking him and hurried outside, where she stood gazing longingly out at the sea, wondering what to do.

At a quarter to seven the sleek black limousine slid to a halt in front of the hotel. The chauffeur, seeing Etta, got out and stood by the car, waiting for her instructions.

Slowly Etta walked up to him, even then not sure what she was going to do. Would she tell him that she would arrange for her luggage to be brought down at once?

Instead, to her great surprise, she found herself saying that she would not need the limousine, that she would be staying at the hotel. He bowed, obviously puzzled, got back in the driving seat and drove off. Etta suppressed an urge to run after him and wave to him to stop. She could not understand it. What had made her change her mind? Had it been Mrs Owens who had made her feel that she was doing a worthwhile job, or had it been the sight of Kaan?

It didn't matter, because the limousine was out of sight now and she was committed to staying with the tour. She turned back to the hotel and halted, surprised to see Kaan by the door and realised he must have seen the scene with the chauffeur.

'I decided to stay,' she said abruptly.

His golden eyes looked into hers. 'I'm glad,' was all he said, but suddenly she was exhilarated, sure that she had made the right decision.

★ ★ ★

That evening the tables were buzzing with discussion about the previous night's robbery. One man had heard that it was not just the jeweller's ordinary stock that had been stolen.

'Apparently someone who was taking some valuable jewels from Istanbul down to the south broke his journey at Kusadasi, and arranged with the jeweller to put his precious stones in his safe for the night. They were all taken.'

'Then someone must have known they would be there,' another man pointed out.

'Well, it wasn't the courier or the jeweller. They were the two men who were injured. The police haven't much hope of finding the jewels. A handful can be worth a fortune, but they can be hidden away very easily.'

'But the robbers were seen by the men they attacked. That will give the police a lead.'

'Oh, yes, the police think they know who they are, and they've been trying desperately to find them before the thieves can get rid of their loot, which is why we had that awful traffic hold-up.'

When the coach left the hotel early the next morning Kaan told those who enquired that he had heard that the robbers had been caught, but the jewels had not been recovered.

'The rumour is that the robbers say they were told to leave the jewels in a rubbish bin a little way from the jeweller's shop and that they'd find a load of cash there as payment. Of course they say they don't know who had made the arrangement or who was going to collect the precious stones. Anyway, the jewels were gone when the police went to look at the bin, but the thieves were carrying a lot of cash.'

'I suppose we'll never know what happens next,' someone said resignedly, and the topic of the robbery was dropped as they began discussing their next stop.

That morning involved a visit to a little-known temple of Aphrodite which delighted those interested in ancient Greek myths. Then in contrast, they carried on to Pamukkale, a geological curiosity where calcium-rich water had, through the centuries, covered the ground in a white sheet which looked at first sight like snow.

Eagerly the tourists spread out along

the paths and cameras were soon busy recording the dazzling white hillsides, but Etta saw that John Burke and Geoff Hunt had, within minutes, found a bench near a café and were sitting looking extremely bored. She felt a pang of pity for those who were not stirred by the unique landscape and went over to speak to them, hoping to convey some of her own enthusiasm.

'Isn't it amazing?' she said, waving an arm at the spectacle.

'I suppose so,' John Burke replied listlessly. Hunt didn't even bother to reply but sat silently holding his shoulder-bag and gazing blankly into the distance. She addressed him directly, determined to get some reaction.

'Don't you like it, Mr Hunt?'

'It's no different to any hill with snow on it, is it?'

She grew impatient. These two were hopeless! 'What did you expect to see when you came here?'

There was no reply. She waited until it became obvious that he would say nothing more, and then strode away feeling definitely annoyed. No matter how bored they were, they could at least have been polite!

However, at that moment one of the tourists approached her, asking if she would take a photograph of her and her husband posed against the white backdrop.

'Isn't it beautiful?' said the woman, wide-eyed. 'I've never seen anything like it.' She thanked Etta once the picture had been taken. 'You know, we've always been on beach holidays before,' she confided, 'but Jack, my husband, said that for once he wanted to see the country, not just the beaches. I'm so glad we came. Of course, the tour costs more than a holiday by the sea, but it's definitely worth it.'

Etta felt much better. What did it matter if a couple of silly men weren't interested in the chance to see this unique and beautiful landscape? She and Kaan were helping people to enjoy an experience which was a special event in their lives, something which justified spending what was to most of them a very large amount of money.

She glanced back at the bench where Burke and Hunt had been sitting, but it was empty. As she looked around to see where they had gone, Kaan came up to her.

'I saw those two men walking away from here. I don't want them to get lost so I'm going to follow them. Will you keep an eye on the rest?'

'Of course. At least they'll be getting some exercise, even if they are not interested in the views.'

'They were striding out as if they knew where they were going, not just wandering around.'

'Kaan, there's definitely something odd about them.'

He sighed. 'Sometimes I think there is something odd about at least half our clients. Anyway, I'll try and make sure they get back on time.'

Etta took more photographs for tourists, agreed that the spectacle was amazing, and told various couples where coffee and the toilets could be found. She saw the young couple, Mary and Gavin, wandering around.

'Are you enjoying today?' she asked them.

'Yes!' they chorused. Gavin said it with real enthusiasm, but Mary had responded dutifully, and Etta laughed.

'But you've seen enough now?' she said to the girl, who smiled guiltily but nodded. She noticed that, unlike on other days, the pair were not holding hands as they walked around. Well, maybe they thought the white covering that looked like snow would be as slippery as snow — but it seemed more likely that something was wrong between them.

Suddenly David Trowbridge accosted her. 'Where's the other rep? Has he left you to cope with us all by yourself?'

She shook her head. 'He went after those two men, Burke and Hunt. He was afraid they would get lost.'

David Trowbridge's face seemed to

sharpen. 'He's following them, seeing where they go?'

'He's just looking after them, doing what he's supposed to do,' she said defensively, but at that moment she saw Kaan coming back, by himself. 'Did you find them?' she asked him, but he shook his head.

'The pair of them seem to have vanished. I just hope they reappear at the coach when it's time to leave.' He turned to David Trowbridge. 'Can we help you?'

But Trowbridge, his face once again relaxed and urbane, shook his head briefly. 'I'm afraid I was just taking the opportunity to talk to our charming rep,' he remarked. 'I'll leave her to you now.'

Kaan frowned, watching Trowbridge walk away. 'If he tries to get too close, too familiar, tell me and I'll have a word with him.'

Etta had been enjoying Trowbridge's obvious admiration and her tone was sharp. 'He was just trying to be friendly, and anyway I can deal with him. I don't need looking after.'

Kaan grinned. 'You're learning rapidly, I'll give you that. Just remember that I'm here to help if you do need me. I certainly don't want to have to face your formidable mother if anything happens to you.'

★　★　★

When it was time for the coach to leave everyone was there, including Burke and Hunt. Etta ostentatiously ticked each name and gave the list to Kaan.

'All present and correct.'

The drive to their hotel in the next town went smoothly, but as they disembarked from the coach and checked in, there was the sound of urgent sirens and squealing tyres from nearby streets.

Over dinner, Kaan informed everybody that he had learned from the hotel staff that there had been yet another robbery — a bank raid this time.

'The robbers weren't after the bank's money apparently. They broke into some strong boxes. The bank doesn't know what's kept in most of them and so is trying to contact the people who have hired the boxes to try and find out what was taken. A lot of the people are furious, but are refusing to say what was kept there. Quite often it's stuff they don't want their families or the taxman to know about.'

'But why did they leave the money?' one woman asked. 'Wouldn't taking cash be easier than having to sell whatever they find in the boxes?'

Her neighbour shook his head knowingly. 'The bank will have a record of the numbers of most of the notes it is holding. That makes them easy to trace.' He expanded on the topic. 'A lot of bank robbers have found out the hard way that you can have hundreds of thousands of pounds in notes and not be able to spend any of it. Laundering the money is difficult if you haven't got the right connections.'

'Fancy having two robberies in two days, in the places we are visiting! Well, I hope there aren't any robberies in the rest of the sites we're going to, or the police will begin to suspect us!'

Etta had remembered that she was running out of toothpaste. The hotel was in a quiet side street, but there were shops a short distance away where she could buy what she needed. But as she went towards the door a voice stopped her in her tracks.

'Etta! At last! I was beginning to think I must have come to the wrong hotel.'

She turned slowly. A tall slender man of about thirty stood a short distance away, smiling at her. He had thick blond hair and blue eyes, and was very good-looking, though with a hint of weakness about the mouth. His cream flannel trousers and blue blazer were obviously expensive, his shoes hand-made.

Etta's first reaction was to think that her mother must have sent this messenger, but then she realised that her parent would never have entrusted such an important errand to this particular individual.

'Miles Standing,' Etta said resignedly. 'And what are you doing here?'

'Need you ask?' He came closer and took her hands in his, smiling confidently down at her as if expecting her to welcome him warmly. 'I've come to give you another chance to do what you really want to, Etta.' He released one hand and brushed a stray lock of hair away from her forehead. 'You look tired, my love. Has it been a long day shepherding a group of strangers around the tourist sights? You know you're just being stubborn. Now let me take you back to your mother.'

She looked at him suspiciously, pulling her other hand away. 'How did you know I was here? How do you know my mother wants me back? She would never have asked you to come to see me.'

Miles Standish shrugged. 'I ran into them at the yacht club yesterday evening. Apparently you were supposed to arrive in their limousine but it came back empty and your mother was furious. So I had a word with their chauffeur and he told me the whole story. Then I did a little checking, found out where you would be, and — well, here I am.'

'And you felt so sorry for my mother that you decided to come all this way to see me, sure that you could charm me into going back with you?'

His smile broadened. 'Almost. I admit it did seem a long way to come, and I wasn't sure if even my charms would be any use if you could say no to your mother face to face. But I followed you here because it occurred to me that you might have refused to join your mother and George on the yacht because you thought you would be bored with just the two oldies, and I remembered how the two of us had enjoyed each other's company that trip we had together.

'If I take you back with me, your mother will feel obliged to ask me to join the three of you on board, then you and I could spend a few pleasant weeks together, just like old times.'

Etta looked at him cynically. 'In other words, you were hoping for a free holiday. What's the matter, Miles? Have you run out of money again? Perhaps another run of bad luck gambling?'

The smile disappeared. He seized her by her arms, and this time his grip was tight and painful. 'Don't be stupid! I'm doing us both a favour. You can't possibly want to stay with this pathetic crowd. All right, I admit I could do with a few quiet weeks at sea away from all those people who claim I owe them money. My car's outside, so come with me now!'

She struggled to free herself. 'Let me go! You're hurting me!'

'Will you please let the lady go?'

It was Mr Edwards who had

intervened, an elderly tourist whom Etta had seen talking to Mrs Dankworth earlier — though to Etta's relief, she was not with him now.

Miles Standish tried to ignore him, but Mr Edwards, in spite of his age, would not desert Etta. Stern and determined, he faced the younger man. 'Let her go — now!'

'Let me go or I'll scream!'

People were looking at them, and Miles Standish, knowing he had lost, released Etta and strode furiously out of the hotel, nearly knocking Mr Edwards over.

Etta put out a hand to support herself on the back of a chair, suddenly realising that she felt very shaky. Mr Edwards, having regained his own balance, hesitantly patted her on the back until she pulled herself upright and managed a smile.

'I'm all right now.'

He still hovered anxiously near her.

'Thank you so much for coming to my aid and, please, don't tell anyone about this incident. It would be very embarrassing for me. It was all a just a silly misunderstanding.'

'Of course I won't say anything,' Mr Edwards said. 'I'm just glad I could help. Are you sure you can manage now?'

She nodded. 'I'm just going to do a bit of shopping. And thank you again.'

Reassured, he walked away, obviously pleased by the success of his gallant intervention. She hurried out of the hotel, eager to complete her errand, but she had only gone a few yards when her arm was seized again.

'There's no geriatric to interfere now, and my car's here, so get in it and stop playing the fool! You're not impressing anyone by pretending you want to stay here, and I need some goodwill from your mother.'

It was Miles Standish again, his face ugly with fury, and he was dragging her towards a sports car. She struggled to free herself, but he was stronger, and when she opened her mouth to call for help he clamped his free hand across it.

'Stop!'

Suddenly Kaan was there, his voice and stance challenging Miles, who was forced to release Etta so that he could face this new opponent.

'And who are you?' he sneered. 'The other travel rep? Well, you don't have to play the hero. She'd never look twice at you.'

Kaan took a step forward, fists clenched, and for a moment it looked as if the two men would come to blows.

Etta thrust herself between them. 'Miles, get out of here now! I am not coming with you, and if you don't leave this instant I shall call Mother and tell her how you've behaved. Then you'll really be in trouble!'

He gave her a long stare, turned on his heel and without a word climbed into his car, started it, and drove away rapidly.

Etta rubbed her arm. There would be a bruise. She found herself blinking back tears. 'It was lucky you came along,' she murmured in an uncertain voice.

Kaan's arms went round her and she relaxed in their comforting strength.

'It wasn't luck,' he said. 'Mr Edwards saw me and told me someone was threatening you, so I came after you to make sure you were safe. Do you want me to call the police? After all, he was virtually trying to kidnap you.'

She considered this offer briefly, shuddered at the idea of the inquisition she would have to face, and shook her head firmly. She felt Kaan relax, and realised how much trouble a police enquiry would have caused the tour firm.

'He won't try it again,' Etta said confidently. 'He must have been desperate to try this time.'

'Well, if you're sure. But I suggest that you really need a coffee after that,' Kaan said firmly. 'Let's go back to the hotel.'

'I need to get some toothpaste first — that's where I was going — then I'll be glad of a coffee.'

With Kaan as escort, the errand was finally completed successfully, and back at the hotel Etta told him what she knew about Miles Standish.

'He was a guest on the yacht once. I told you Mother was always looking for a suitable partner for me, and Miles can be very charming. He also has some rich relatives, so Mother thought he would be just right for me.' She avoided his eyes. 'I admit I did find him attractive for a time, but then I realised all he cared about was finding ways to use people for his own benefit. Then Mother discovered that he's the black sheep of the family, a gambler, so he was never invited again.'

'He was taking a big risk today to please your mother.'

'I think he must be desperate. He doesn't just *like* gambling, he's compulsive. Perhaps he's lost everything, and this was a last-ditch attempt to save himself.'

Kaan shuddered. 'I've seen such a

compulsion — to gamble or to drink — destroy people completely. In a way I pity them, and I'm very glad I'm not like them.'

4

As they left the lounge the head waiter approached Kaan, looking a little worried, and told him that they had been keeping a check on the diners as they had come for their evening meal. Two of the tour's clients had not yet appeared for dinner, and the restaurant would soon be closing.

The culprits proved, not unexpectedly, to be Burke and Hunt. There was no answer from their room so they were obviously out somewhere in the town.

'If they miss dinner, it's their own fault,' Kaan said resignedly, 'and I'll tell them so. They know what time we are supposed to eat.'

In fact they saw the two culprits strolling in casually at that very moment.

'I'm afraid you're too late to have

dinner in the hotel,' Kaan said with icy politeness.

Burke shrugged. 'That's all right. We've had a meal. We decided to eat out, to get away from everybody.'

'Why didn't you tell me?' said an exasperated Kaan, but they looked at him blankly.

'Does it matter if we miss a meal? We don't want any money back,' Burke told him.

'We'd had enough of all the oldies chattering on. It's a relief to get away from them for an hour or so,' Hunt added.

Kaan bit his lip to restrain a sharp rejoinder and retreated to the lounge where Etta was waiting to hear what had happened.

'You know, they're behaving more and more peculiarly,' she said after he had reported the encounter.

'They are bad-mannered, thoughtless and bored, that's all.' He looked at her sharply. 'Don't go imagining anything else. I've seen it all before.'

There was the sound of yet another police siren outside. Kaan cocked his head and smiled. 'Well, whatever the reason is for their behaviour, at least you can't suspect them of being involved in the robbery. That happened before we got here.'

⋆ ⋆ ⋆

It was a long drive the next day, one that impressed Etta with the scale and variety of Turkey's landscape as they drove through fertile fields, busy towns and past towering mountains.

'I hadn't realised Turkey was so big! In England we would have driven from one end of the country to the other by now,' she marvelled.

'And remember, you're only seeing a small part of the west of Turkey,' Kaan pointed out.

Most of their fellow-travellers seemed to enjoy the restful drive after the intensive sight-seeing of the past few days. By now they had sorted themselves into small groups. Mrs Dankworth, rather surprisingly, seemed to have forged a firm friendship with the elegant woman in her seventies, Valerie Pritchard, who was also travelling on her own, and Etta had noticed that her own personal saviour, Mr Edwards, was often to be seen escorting the two ladies.

But Etta was a little worried when she saw Mary West sitting silent and glum, staring out of the window with her back turned pointedly to her partner while Gavin Preston talked to his neighbours. When he did make an effort to include her in the conversation from time to time, Mary coldly ignored him, as she had at other times.

'Let's hope she gets over being miserable soon, or she'll spoil it for both of them,' was Kaan's comment when Etta pointed out what was happening. But he was to be disappointed.

They arrived at their hotel in mid-afternoon and most of the tourists decided they were rested enough to go out and explore the ancient town of Konya. Etta was sitting in the lounge, reading an old English newspaper she had found and catching up on the week-old news, when she looked up and found Mary West standing in front of her, looking very pale and agitated.

'Oh, I'm sorry,' Etta said, hastily putting down the paper. 'I was miles away. Can I help you?'

'Yes,' said Mary desperately. 'I want to go home!'

Etta frowned. She must have misheard the girl. 'I'm sorry?'

'I want to go home!'

'Home?'

'Yes. To England. I want to go home now!'

She seemed on the edge of tears as Etta stared at her. 'You want to go back now? You and Gavin? What's the matter? Have you had bad news?'

'Gavin doesn't want to go, just me. And nothing's happened at home but I want to go back — today if I can!'

The tears started to pour down her

face as she sobbed loudly. Etta scrambled to her feet and put her arm round the girl, looking round anxiously, relieved to see that there were no witnesses to Mary's distress.

'Oh, don't cry, Mary. We can sort out the problem, whatever it is. Now let's go in here so we can talk.'

She hastily led Mary into a small room next to the main office and shut the door. There were two upright chairs and a desk, so she sat the girl down in one chair and perched herself on a corner of the desk and handed her tissues. She waited until Mary had stopped crying and started sniffing miserably. Finally she gave a great sigh and blew her nose loudly.

'Now, tell me all about it,' Etta said coaxingly, and found that Mary was only too eager to pour out her woes.

'It was Gavin who wanted to come on a holiday. I didn't want to spend the money. You see, I've always wanted a big wedding, a day to remember for the rest of my life, and that takes a lot of arranging and it's going to cost a lot of money, of course. But I was perfectly happy to do without things if it meant I could have my dream wedding.'

She sniffed loudly again before going on. 'But Gavin said he was fed up with never going anywhere because we were saving every penny we could, and he went on and on until finally I agreed we'd have a few days away. Then I found he'd booked this tour because he's interested in history — I wanted a nice hotel by a beach — and this costs more! We could have spent the extra money on our wedding.'

Etta made comforting noises. 'The hotels are comfortable in Turkey, and there is a lot to see and enjoy,' she pointed out, but Mary shot her a scornful look.

'But it's just old ruins and they're not even romantic! Gavin spends more time looking at things and reading about them than he does paying attention to me.' She bent her head and Etta had to crane to hear her muffled voice. 'And being with Gavin isn't what I'd expected. He snores and makes noises . . . ' To Etta's relief she stopped there.

'You mean he's human,' she said gently. 'I expect he might say you have your faults as well.'

Mary gave her an indignant glare. This was clearly not the sympathy and sisterly support she had expected. Etta sighed and broke the bad news.

'Well, I'm sorry to disappoint you, but I'm afraid you can't fly back to England from here anyway. There isn't an international airport locally. You'll have to wait until we reach Istanbul, and by then the holiday will be nearly over. You'll just have to be patient for a few more days. Surely you can do that.'

But Mary was crying again, snuffling into the sodden tissue.

'Where's Gavin now? Does he know you want to leave?' Etta asked patiently.

'No. He went out to look round the town. I told him I didn't want to, that old towns were boring, but he still went. That was the last straw, so I came looking for you!'

Etta saw a gleam of hope. If Gavin was unaware of the crisis, maybe Mary could be persuaded to keep quiet and think about her situation and then she might possibly change her mind about her impulsive decision to leave.

'Why don't you go up to your room, wash your face and try to calm down? As I said, we can't do anything till we get to Istanbul, so if I were you I wouldn't say anything to Gavin about wanting to leave him just yet. It would make for a very uncomfortable few days if he knew.' Etta frowned. 'I suppose you realise you will have to pay quite a bit extra for a special flight home. A pity, but at least you won't be saving up for the wedding any longer.'

Mary looked at her blankly. 'Why not?'

'Well, if you leave him like this, Gavin will be sure to call it off even if you don't.'

Mary reacted with horror. She had

obviously imagined herself flying off to England and leaving behind a heartbroken Gavin who would have learned his lesson and in future do exactly as he was told once they were reunited. Now it was being pointed out that her impulsive action might lose her both Gavin *and* her dream wedding day. She was looking very thoughtful as Etta saw her into the lift.

'Trouble with young love's dream?' a voice enquired. It was Valerie Pritchard, the lady who'd made friends with Mrs Dankworth. She laughed at Etta's expression and patted her arm. 'Don't worry, dear. It's all right. I'm not going to ask for details, but it's been pretty clear from the start of the tour that the girl wasn't happy.'

She patted her perfectly-groomed white hair. 'In the past I have had a number of what are now called relationships, and I decided long ago that you should never go on holiday with a lover. The intimacy of sharing a room soon ruins romance. These days I settle for friendship. It's much more peaceful.'

'Are you thinking of Mr Edwards?' Etta dared to enquire.

Valerie Pritchard smiled a little smugly. 'So you've noticed? I have my hopes . . . '

Etta went to find Kaan, who listened to her account with masculine exasperation, his sympathies clearly with Gavin.

'So she wants everything her way, she wants that poor young man to dedicate every minute to her, and instead he's dared to show an interest in Turkey as well as her. What a pain!'

Etta tried to defend Mary. 'Basically she's a nice, pleasant girl. It's just that she feels her dream day is being put in jeopardy for the sake of a holiday she isn't enjoying.'

'She's made no attempt to enjoy it!'

Etta had nothing to say to this because it was obviously true.

'Oh well, I suppose we could get separate rooms for them,' Kaan said grudgingly, 'but they'd have to pay extra and put up with a lot of gossip. I'll try and catch Gavin when he comes in and have a man-to-man talk, tell him to be a bit more attentive, though I won't tell him his girlfriend is planning to leave him.' He groaned at the prospect. 'I'm glad I was never romantic.'

'No,' Etta returned tartly. 'Your approach was to knock on the bedroom door, clutching a bottle of wine.'

He grinned and looked at her challengingly. 'What would you do if I knocked on your door?'

She looked at him uncertainly. Was he being serious? It was impossible to tell. She decided to treat it as a joke. 'Take the bottle of wine, thank you for it, then close the door firmly in your face,' she retorted finally.

He was laughing openly now. 'Would you? Am I really so unattractive to you?'

He took her hand and looked into her eyes but she could see nothing but amusement in the golden gaze, an awareness of his masculine challenge.

She snatched her hand free. 'Stop flirting, Kaan. You're my boss and my teacher, and you've put me through some very awkward moments in the last few days. I'm never going to feel romantic about you.'

He was laughing again. 'You know, my mother would approve of you, Etta.' He looked round sharply as the door opened. 'Here comes Gavin now! I'll grab him before he goes upstairs and talk to him like a father or an agony aunt. Well, a free drink may help him listen.'

He made off purposefully and Etta saw him take the young man by the arm and draw him towards the bar. She decided she had had enough for one night of young love's problems and went up to her room without waiting to see what happened.

Later, curled up in bed with the guide book, checking on the next day's route, she heard a gentle knock on her door and jerked upright. She realised she had been half-listening for a tap on her door which would prove to be Kaan waiting outside, come to call her bluff. Would she let him in? He was very attractive — and he knew it!

Slowly she swung her legs to the floor and went to the door, opening it just a crack, conscious that her heart was thumping. But instead of Kaan she saw Valerie Pritchard, who apologised for disturbing her but who wanted to check what time they would leave the next day. Etta told her and returned to bed, wondering what she would have done if it had been Kaan . . .

She'd have slammed the door in his face! Of course she would! But she could not forget how she had felt in the comfort of his arms after he had faced down Miles Standing . . . and then she found herself imagining them tightening round her in passion. She thumped her pillow in disgust.

The sleep she badly needed finally came an hour later.

*   *   *

Whatever Kaan had said to Gavin, it seemed to have some effect, because Mary was not looking quite so miserable the next morning. She even seized a moment to murmur quietly to Etta that she hadn't said anything to Gavin about leaving him — yet. Fortunately the day was to be spent admiring the fairy-tale landscape of Cappadocia, where fantastic edifices created from great hollowed-out cones of rock dominated the landscape. Surely even Mary would find them fascinating?

Watching her, Etta thought at first that the girl was interested. Only for a time, unfortunately. Mary obviously grew tired of climbing steep flights of rough stone steps and Etta heard her complaining shrilly to Gavin that he should wait for her instead of rushing ahead to look at yet another lump of rock.

Etta saw Gavin apparently apologising for his lack of thought and trying to put his arm round his sweetheart, but Mary pushed him away bad-temperedly. Taken by surprise, Gavin stumbled and fell heavily. As Mary screamed, horrified by what she had done, he rolled helplessly down a steep slope and crashed into a rock, where he gave a cry of pain and lay there, apparently unable to move.

Etta hurried recklessly towards him as fast as she could, leaping down steps, careless of her own safety. When she reached Gavin she was relieved to see that he was at least conscious, trying to pull himself upright, but he looked dazed and grasped his right arm, wincing with pain, until finally he gave up the effort and slumped back against the rock.

As Etta reached him Mary slid down the slope and flung herself down beside him, full of remorse, crying out how sorry she was. Etta pushed her gently aside so that she could check what was wrong with him.

'What's the matter, Gavin? Tell me what's hurting,' Etta demanded.

He shook his head as if to clear it before replying and tentatively moved his arm. 'I hit my elbow, so that's hurting like mad, though I bent my wrist back as well.' He tried to move his hand, but stopped in obvious pain.

'Let me look,' said Etta, blocking Mary's attempts to embrace Gavin and blessing the first-aid course the travel firm had insisted she take a few weeks before. She took his arm and felt along it cautiously.

Gavin tensed. 'That's where it hurts.'

Etta frowned, gently touching the area he had indicated and saw him flinch. 'It looks as if you've sprained your wrist, as well as damaging your elbow, so we need to get you to a doctor,' was her verdict.

Disregarding Mary's wails, she took off the white cotton scarf she wore round her neck and began to fashion a sling to support his hand and lower arm. Before she had time to finish this task, Kaan had arrived, alerted by another member of the party who had seen the accident.

As he knelt by Gavin, Etta explained her diagnosis and he also checked and then nodded. 'I agree. Don't worry, we'll soon get you to a doctor, Gavin. It's not far to the car park. Do you think you can walk there if we help you?' he asked.

'My legs are all right, just a bit scratched. It's only my arm that really hurts — nothing else.' As if to contradict this he winced as Kaan put an arm round him and gently helped him to his feet. 'Though I may have a few bruises here and there.' Gavin added ruefully.

'You're doing well,' Kaan said encouragingly. 'There are always taxis dropping people off at the car park and there's a local doctor who has helped us before with minor accidents so Etta can take you to him. I'll call him on my mobile to tell him to expect you.'

'I'm going too!' Mary exclaimed shrilly. 'He's my fiancé and it was my fault. I must stay with him.'

Kaan shrugged.

'No problem.' He turned back to Etta. 'I'll wait until you get a taxi, then I'll come back and look after the rest of the party, and I'll see you all back at the hotel later.'

As he had predicted, it was easy to find a taxi that had just deposited some sightseers and was glad of a return fare. Gavin sat in the back supported by Etta and Mary, the latter full of tearful remorse. Gavin told her she shouldn't blame herself for the accident — a far more forgiving response than she would have received had Etta spoken her mind.

Back in town, the taxi took them to the address which Kaan had given the driver and they were rapidly ushered into a waiting-room. Within a minute the doctor came in to greet them. He was a pleasant, plumpish man, but Etta was aware less of what he looked like and more of his tie, which was a garish array of vivid colours depicting various cartoon characters. She had never seen a professional man wearing such a garish thing, and was aware of how her eyes kept returning to it as she explained what had happened. Etta and Mary then waited while Gavin was taken by the doctor into his consulting-room, though Mary had protested at being excluded from the doctor's examination.

'We are going to be married. I have a right to stay with him,' she announced, and Etta had to bite her lip to stop herself from reminding the girl that only a few hours before she had been eager to leave Gavin.

'Stay with me, Mary,' Etta told the girl firmly. 'You'll only distract the doctor.'

The young man emerged twenty minutes later smiling happily and wearing a much more efficient-looking bandage.

'You were right. The young man has hurt his wrist, but not badly, and he has a bruised elbow,' the doctor informed Etta. 'I have strapped him up and told him when he can take the bandage off.'

While Mary fussed over Gavin, Etta thanked the doctor.

'I'm afraid I'm new to this,' she confessed. 'I mean, about paying? What happens next?'

The doctor waved an airy hand. 'Don't worry. There is a well-established procedure.' He saw that she was staring at his tie once again, and he smiled mischievously. 'You like my tie?'

She hesitated, torn between politeness and truth, and his smile grew broader.

'I wear it because it distracts people from their pain and discomfort. If it doesn't, I know they are really having trouble. My wife hates it, incidentally.'

While his receptionist called a taxi, Etta thanked him again. 'It was a silly little accident. I'm sorry we had to bother you.'

The doctor looked sideways to where Mary was tenderly helping Gavin towards the door. 'My part is the easy one,' he said. 'I just have to deal with the physical troubles. You have to deal with the personal problems, and that can be a much more difficult task.'

She smiled at him. 'You know, I think for once the physical problem may have helped with the personal problems.'

★ ★ ★

The three returned to the hotel to find the coach had arrived with the rest of the party a short time before, and over dinner some tourists commiserated with Gavin, telling him what splendours he had missed in the second part of the visit. Gavin sighed, but did not look too depressed.

Mary was still fussing over him, rushing to fulfil his slightest wish, cutting up his meat and making sure he had exactly what he wanted. It was clear that after her recent coldness he was enjoying being looked after like this, and thought a sore wrist and a few bruises a small price to pay.

Gavin's accident was, of course, the

main topic of conversation when Kaan and Etta settled to review the day's events after dinner.

'Obviously Mary is feeling very guilty,' Etta commented. 'After all, technically she did push him over, but she didn't mean to and he wasn't badly hurt. Now she feels it is her fault and is desperately trying to please him, and that won't leave her any time to feel bored and start brooding or wanting to leave him, so I think they'll both be here for the end of the tour.'

She sighed heavily. 'I wonder what will happen when they get back to England?'

'They'll probably carry on just as they did before they came to Turkey,' was Kaan's opinion. 'I wouldn't be surprised if we were even invited to the wedding!'

'But she wanted to leave him and go home!'

'He doesn't know that, and the fact that he likes ancient history and she doesn't isn't going to cause much trouble in their day-to-day life in England, though it may complicate deciding where to go for their holidays.'

Etta heaved a sigh. 'We'll probably never know what happens to them.' She looked sadly at Kaan. 'Don't you feel frustrated when you meet all these people for a few days, learn all about them, and then don't know what happens to them afterwards?'

It occurred to her with a shock that this would apply to the two of them as well as to their clients. In six months' time, would she be in contact with Kaan? Would he care if they parted in Istanbul and never met again?

Kaan was shaking his head. 'That's what life is like. How many old school friends did you swear to keep in touch with, and how many do you have anything to do with now? All those neighbours and acquaintances who were so important in your life — do you know what happened to them after you moved?'

She was silent for a while. 'I suppose

it's true that we have very few life-long relationships,' she said at last. She shuddered. 'You're making me feel very lonely.'

'Not everybody vanishes,' he said comfortably. 'There's always your family. I left a lot of friends behind in England but I have my mother, two sisters, umpteen aunts and uncles and cousins. I sometimes wish I could lose touch with some of them when they get aggravating or interfering, but at least I know they're there when I need them.'

Etta gazed down at her interlocked fingers. 'I don't have that,' she said quietly. 'There's only my mother. I hardly know my stepfather.'

His voice was sympathetic. 'But she won't always be the only one,' he said. 'You aren't limited to the family Fate gave you. Most people choose a partner for life, someone they can love and who loves them. They support each other and stop each other feeling lonely. I know you haven't met anyone like that so far, and neither have I, but I'm sure we will. I hope so, anyway. My parents had a very happy marriage, and I hope to have one like theirs.' His tone changed as if he felt he had revealed too much of his private feelings. 'Anything else we should discuss?'

Etta shook her head.

'Good. Nearly bedtime again, I'm afraid.'

'I'll go up to my room now. It's been another full day.'

He stretched out a hand to detain Etta as she rose. 'Incidentally, I haven't congratulated you on the way you handled Gavin's accident this morning. You didn't panic and you coped admirably. I'd have been in trouble if I'd had to look after him and the rest of the party on my own. Thank you.'

She went off feeling pleased and proud. Kaan's opinion was becoming important to her and he had just revealed another side of himself . . . he was a man who believed in life-long love, the happy, permanent companion-ship of a man and a woman.

She tried to imagine him surrounded by his family and envied his sisters as she compared his steady life to her own succession of frustrated attempts to form relationships as her mother had repeatedly moved from one husband to another.

She felt she was getting on better with the members of the group also, that they no longer regarded her as just the girl who trailed along after Kaan but as a competent member of the touring staff, and they were much more friendly.

There were exceptions, of course. John Burke and Geoff Hunt still ignored her, but she consoled herself with the thought that they also ignored every other member of the party. Soon she discovered that this behaviour was annoying somebody else. Passing along the hotel corridor on her way to Reception, she heard a voice raised in anger and realised that it was coming from one of the rooms whose door was not quite shut. She stopped, her attention caught by what she heard.

'What do you think you are playing at?' the speaker demanded. 'You're supposed to be ordinary tourists, enjoying your holiday. Instead you're making it absolutely obvious that you're bored stiff and can't wait to get the whole thing over.'

There was a reply, the tone resentful, though Etta could not catch the words. The first speaker went on.

'I don't care how you feel. Now make an effort. Speak to a few people, show an interest in the places we visit.'

There was another murmur, to which the speaker replied, 'I'm going now, but I'll be watching you.'

Etta sped down the passage on tiptoe. She heard the door open and risked peering back along the corridor. She saw a man's back as he made for the stairs. The back and the voice were instantly recognisable. It was David Trowbridge — and she knew the room he had just come out of had been assigned to Burke and Hunt.

Obviously she would have to report this odd little incident to Kaan and see what he made of it. When she went back downstairs she saw him in the reception area, but before she could attract his attention she felt a hand on her arm, and was taken aback to find that it was David Trowbridge himself who was detaining her.

'Miss Sanderson,' he smiled, 'I wanted to congratulate you on the way you handled that young man's accident.'

There was no trace of the anger she had heard in his voice a few minutes earlier. She thanked him and went to walk on, but apparently he had more to say.

'I was told that you're not really a travel rep, that you're just on this trip to see how the tours are run. Has it made you feel that you'd like to become a full-time rep?'

'I'm not sure,' she said politely, feeling a little wary. 'It's a demanding job.'

'But it could be very rewarding, I hear. I'm not talking about the pay — though I'm sure that's adequate — but reps are moving through the country freely and people get to know them and see them as people they can trust, so you needn't be just a rep . . . you could . . . do things for people, along the way.'

'I'm not sure that's allowed,' she said uncertainly, wondering what exactly he was talking about.

'Who'd know? Anyway, I'll be interested to hear if you do decide to come on any more trips. I might even join you again. It could be to our mutual advantage.'

With that he left her. His hints about the future were puzzling. What on earth could they do together to their 'mutual advantage'? Did he already have reps helping him — and if so what exactly did they do for him?

She found Kaan still in the lounge and detached him from the people he was talking to as quickly as possible.

'I thought you were going to bed. What's the emergency?' he enquired. 'You were almost rude to that couple.'

'I'm sorry, but there's something I have to tell you.' She poured out her story and her suspicions. Kaan was silent when she finished and she waited impatiently. 'Well?' she challenged him at last.

'I don't know. You may be right, but Trowbridge could say he was only making conversation and didn't mean anything by it.'

'But what about what he was saying to Burke and Hunt in their room?'

'Perhaps he just got fed up with the way they behave and decided to give them a piece of his mind.'

'But why did he think he had the right to talk to them like that — and why did they listen instead of just throwing him out of their room?'

'Perhaps they knew they'd been rude and he was entitled to lose his patience and tell them what he thought of them.' She gave an impatient snort and he held up his hand. 'All right! I agree I can't see them doing that and it is all very suspicious, but we can't accuse them of anything on what we've learned so far. We'll just have to keep a very close eye on them — and that's all we can do.'

She had to agree.

Etta's feelings were mixed as she went back to her room. She had proved her worth when she dealt with Gavin's accident and Kaan had acknowledged that. But it had been a long, demanding day and she was very weary . . . and tomorrow morning she would have to drag herself out of bed and be smart and smiling for the tourists.

But she didn't *have* to do it. Even now, one phone call to her mother and someone would arrive to whisk her away to the yacht, to a life where other people had to worry while she relaxed and enjoyed herself. After all, she had done it before. Why wasn't she ready to walk away this time?

Gazing into the darkness, she was

forced to admit that she might want to escape from people like Mary West, but she didn't want to leave Kaan. He was what was keeping her with the tour.

5

All the tourists were ready for the coach the next morning, and Etta was intrigued to notice that, whereas the two women who had come on their own, Mrs Dankworth and Valerie Pritchard, had been sitting together so far with Mr Edwards seated on his own in front of them, that day Mr Edwards was seated next to Mrs Dankworth. Valerie Pritchard saw Etta looking and smiled and shrugged, spreading her coat and bag over the empty seat beside her.

The coach steadily ate up the miles. Now it was in the second half of the tour and heading for Ankara, Turkey's capital. Etta, used to ancient London as her capital, found it difficult to grasp that a comparatively small town could be suddenly transformed into an important capital city by a government's edict, as Ankara had been. 'Is it all new, then?' she asked Kaan.

'Most of it.' He laughed at her expression of bewilderment. 'Wait and see, and don't have any preconceived ideas.'

It was indeed strange to move from cities thousand of years old, like Troy and Ephesus, to the elegant modernity of Ankara, and Etta found it an interesting contrast as they explored it.

As the coach returned to the hotel that afternoon she was looking forward to discussing what she had seen with Kaan, but when she was helping the tourists disembark an urgent voice claimed her attention.

'So you've come at last. I've been waiting ages!'

She swung round and then peered disbelievingly at the woman who had spoken. It took a second look to confirm that it was indeed her mother in front of her for Etta could scarcely recognise her; she looked so unlike her usual self.

Her calm self-possession had gone,

and she looked very agitated. Instead of her customary elegance and careful grooming, her make-up was carelessly applied and her mascara was smudged as though she had been crying. Her clothes looked as if they had been chosen at random and flung on.

Etta could not remember ever seeing her mother in anything approaching this state. What disaster could have happened in the short time since she had last seen her to make her lose her customary poise so completely? Her heart started pounding.

'I have to speak to you!' her mother said urgently, clutching her daughter's arm.

'What's the matter?' Etta thought of her stepfather and her eyes widened. 'Has something happened to George?'

But instead of replying Mrs Trent was tugging at her, trying to pull her away from the watching tourists.

'Come with me and I'll tell you everything. Come along now!'

Etta looked desperately to Kaan for

guidance and help. He was still busy dealing with the coach passengers, but was obviously aware of her situation because he turned his head and gave her a little nod, an indication that he could cope while she tried to deal with the distraught woman.

'All right, Mother. Where would you like to go?' Etta asked, keeping her voice as calm and level as possible while wincing as her mother's fingers dug into her arm.

Her mother pointed a shaking finger. 'There! There are some gardens. Let's go there so we can talk.'

She was almost trying to drag Etta across the road, regardless of the traffic, and would have stepped out in front of a taxi if Etta had not held her back at the last second. With her mother obviously unable to look after herself, Etta decided that she would have to take charge. She shook herself free of her mother's hand and then quickly linked her arm through that of her parent.

'Let's get there safely,' she said as calmly as she could. 'Now, there's a break in the traffic coming up. Cross now!' Obedient as a child, her mother did as she was told.

When the two of them had reached safety in the little park, Etta looked around and saw a bench in the shade of some trees.

'We can sit here and you can tell me what the trouble is,' she said soothingly, leading her mother towards it and finding it very strange to be the one giving instructions. Her mother almost collapsed on the seat, but then, as Etta sat waiting, instead of speaking Mrs Trent just sat hunched forward, twisting her fingers together and staring into the distance — almost as if she had forgotten Etta's presence.

'Mother?'

Her mother turned to her with a jerk.

'We collected some mail this morning,' she said with apparent irrelevance, and then stopped.

'Yes?' Etta said encouragingly once it

149

was clear her mother was not going to continue without prompting.

'There was one for me — it had been addressed to our home but then forwarded. It was from a woman I knew a long time ago. We used to send each other the occasional Christmas card but I haven't really had anything to do with her for years.'

She was silent again and Etta waited patiently.

'I haven't heard from her since I married George. I don't know how she found my address.' More silence.

'Why did she write to you?' Etta said at last.

'She thought I ought to know . . . she thought that perhaps I should tell you . . . ' Mrs Trent sat up and stared at Etta. 'She thought we should know that your father is dead,' she said flatly. Etta looked at her blankly and a touch of her mother's usual impatience reappeared. 'You know — Harry Sanderson. Your father. He's died.'

It was the first time she had spoken

his name to Etta in years. 'My father? What happened to him?'

Her mother shrugged. 'Some virus. He didn't go to the doctor till it was too late. Typical.'

Suddenly her hands were covering her face as sobs shook her body. Still trying to digest the news, Etta put her arms round her, for the first time in her life trying to comfort her mother.

'It's all right, Mother. There's no reason for you to be upset. He walked out of our lives a long time ago.'

'It was such a shock! I thought I'd managed to put all that behind me, to forget all about that time,' her mother choked.

Etta was completely bewildered. Her mother had always given the impression that her relationship with Etta's father had been a youthful brief mistake, but now she was apparently distraught by the news of his death.

'It all came back to me,' Mrs Trent almost wailed. 'We were so young, everything seemed so wonderful. I thought we would always love each other and we would be together for ever.'

'Do you still love him, after all this time?' Etta asked hesitantly, but her mother shook her head violently.

'No! He deserted me, left me alone when I was pregnant, with no one to turn to. I was desperate but I was determined to survive. So I put all my youthful ideas of romance and love behind me and did what I had to — married a man I didn't love because he could give me security, then another because he could give me — and you — even more.'

Her mother sat up and wiped her eyes angrily with the back of her hand, smearing her mascara even more. 'When I read that letter suddenly everything came back. Don't think I'm crying for Harry Sanderson — I'm not such a fool — I'm crying for the girl I used to be, and what he made me become. I remembered the loneliness and the poverty — going to bed early to keep warm, not always being very clean because it cost too much money to heat water — life was so miserable that sometimes I wondered why I even bothered trying to survive.'

'But there was me.' Etta said quietly. Her mother nodded.

'There was you, the one good thing he left me, the reason I had to survive because you were completely dependent upon me, so I had to live and somehow make sure that you would be safe and warm and fed. I managed it, but it changed me and made me hard. I couldn't afford feelings or weaknesses.'

She buried her face in her hands. 'I gave up a lot for you, and I've never regretted it, but now I've been forced to look back, and I feel so sorry for that poor young girl I used to be!'

The tears came again and she collapsed in Etta's arms and was held for some minutes, her daughter rubbing her back and crooning to her as if she were holding a young child.

Suddenly there was a quiet cough

and Etta looked round sharply. Kaan was standing behind the bench they were sitting on, and with him she saw another, older, white-haired man, dressed in jeans, a short-sleeved shirt and deck shoes.

Etta recognised her stepfather, George Trent. Normally calm and smiling, he was frowning deeply as he looked down at his wife. Now he came round and put his hands gently on his wife's shoulders. 'Come with me, Jane. I'm here to take care of you and the car is waiting.'

Etta's mother looked up at him, tears still visible on her cheeks. 'You don't know what's happened.'

'I know everything. I read the letter. You left it on the table together with the leaflet giving details of Etta's tour, so I was able to follow you.'

'How long have you been standing there? I suppose long enough to hear what I said to Etta, so you know I plotted to attract you, to marry you,' she said bleakly. 'I wanted to be wealthy and secure, and you were a way to achieve that . . . and now you'll despise me.'

George Trent smiled at her tenderly and a little sadly.

'I know, my love,' he said gently, sliding his hands down her arms and starting to lift her up. 'I've always known. I was glad you'd chosen me. I married you because I loved you, and I wanted to make you happy. Now, come along with me and we can talk about everything later when you're feeling better.'

He looked at Etta, who nodded her approval, and then he took a large white handkerchief from his pocket and wiped his wife's eyes. Mrs Trent did not resist when her husband raised her to her feet and put his arm round her, nor did she look at her daughter or say anything more to her.

Kaan and Etta watched as the older woman allowed herself to be led slowly away to the big black car. They saw her almost collapse on the back seat like a rag doll, and then the limousine drove smoothly off. As she lost sight of it Etta closed her eyes and gave a small gasp.

'Are you all right?' Kaan asked urgently. 'No, of course you aren't. Here, sit down again.'

She shook her head. 'No! I need to move, I need to think!'

She began to walk along the path, gradually faster and faster until she was almost running, but Kaan kept pace with her until she stopped suddenly and turned to face him.

'My father's dead!' she said simply, and then the tears began to run down her face.

'He left my mother before I was born so I never met him, and I knew he'd treated my mother badly. But sometimes, when I'd had an argument with my mother, I would have this vague idea that some day we would meet and he would realise what a marvellous daughter I would have been, and then we would get to know each other and care for each other. When my mother seemed harsh and unfeeling I would imagine that was what drove him away, not the prospect of having to be a father, and that we would sympathise with each other and understand each other. And now that's never going to happen.'

Kaan's arms were round her now and he was making soft, wordless noises. She let her head rest on his shoulder. Once again she was comforted by his nearness, by his warmth.

'But it's not only that,' she went on. 'My mother is upset, unhappy, unable to control herself, and I've never seen her like that before. I'm no longer certain about a lot of things I thought I could be sure about.'

'Then come back to the hotel. I'll deal with any tourist problems, and you can have your dinner sent up to your room so that you can have a quiet evening to think things out.'

She let him lead her back to the hotel where she heard him explain to the girl at Reception that Miss Sanderson was not feeling very well, so he would be grateful if she would arrange for tea to be sent to Etta's room straight away, with some food to be sent up later.

Once in her room, she gratefully drank the tea when it arrived, realising anew what a pleasure it was to be alone after a long day in the constant company of others. Then she lay down on the bed fully clothed to think about what had happened. But suddenly she was very, very tired, and her eyes closed and she fell fast asleep.

She was woken by the telephone ringing. Groggily she fumbled for it. Was it Kaan or one of the tourists wanting help?

'Hello?' she managed.

'Etta?' To her amazement she recognised her mother's voice, and it was very obviously not the hesitant broken voice of that afternoon, but once again the usual confident and self-assured tone. 'Have I finally got through to you? That young man you work with seems to be vetting your calls.'

'You mean Kaan Talbot, and it is me, Mother. How are you?'

Her mother must have heard the anxiety and concern in her daughter's voice and there was a momentary hesitation before she replied, 'Perfectly all right, thank you.'

There was a self-conscious laugh. 'Do me a favour and forget about this afternoon. I can't have been feeling well, or I wouldn't have made such a spectacle of myself. Now listen,' she swept on, 'I checked with your Mr Talbot and he insists that you are needed for some excursions tomorrow during the day, but I did get him to agree that he can spare you in the evening.' There was an indignant snort. 'Kind of him! Our car will pick you up from your Istanbul hotel at seven o'clock.'

'What for?'

'Dinner, of course. George and I will be at the Club.'

Emma shook her head, trying to clear it as she tried to reconcile this incisive woman with her last sight of her mother in a state of collapse being led away by George Trent.

'So everything is all right between the two of you?'

There was another pause. 'Of course. Why ever not? We'll see you tomorrow. And Etta . . . '

'Yes?'

'There's no need for you to dress up, but do at least try to look presentable.'

There was a click. The message had been delivered and her mother, as ever, was not going to waste time on unnecessary pleasantries.

Bodily needs were making themselves felt and suddenly Etta became aware of urgent pangs of hunger. She looked at her watch. It was late. Could she still get something to eat downstairs? But when she opened her door she found a tray of cold meats, salad and bread waiting outside. Gratefully she brought the tray in and started to attack the food greedily.

Appetite finally satisfied, she found

herself thinking that she would have to make absolutely sure that Kaan could manage without her tomorrow evening before she went off for dinner at the yacht club, and realised with some surprise that her concern about her work was as important as her mother's commands. She was finally breaking free from her mother's apron strings!

It was too late to do anything but go to bed by then, so Etta stripped and showered and cuddled down for the night. Life was getting more and more interesting. She couldn't wait to find out what had happened between her mother and George Trent to bring about such a rapid transformation.

*   *   *

The next morning, in response to her anxious enquiries, Kaan reassured her there would be no problem with her absence.

'We'll be back in Istanbul and everybody will know the hotel, so it should be a quiet time.' He grinned. 'Anyway, your mother was very firm about wanting you to be free, and I wouldn't dare upset her plans. She certainly does seem to have made a remarkable recovery,' he added. There was a note of interrogation in his voice.

'My stepfather seems to have worked a minor miracle. I'm hoping to find out how tonight.'

'Well, I'd like to know how he did it, too — so long as it's not family matters you'd rather keep to yourself.

'Incidentally, to change the subject, I'm wondering if you were right about Burke and Hunt behaving rather strangely. After doing their best to ignore everybody so far this tour, they suddenly started being very friendly and eager to talk to everyone last night,' Kaan told her.

'You mean they'd thought about what Trowbridge said and decided he had a point?'

'I don't know about that, but I will be

watching their future conduct with interest.'

The tour had come full circle and was returning to Istanbul that day, and to the same hotel as it had started from. To a certain extent that made some of the travellers feel rather sad, because it meant the tour was coming to an end. On the other hand, it would certainly be the highlight of the holiday as the tourists were about to see the most splendid achievements of the Ottoman Empire.

'There's so much in Istanbul!' fretted Valerie Pritchard, clutching her guide book. 'We just can't manage to see everything. It's so frustrating!'

Kaan smiled down at her as he helped her on the coach.

'There is a solution, of course — come back again!'

Mrs Pritchard and Mrs Dankworth were both sitting with empty seats beside them when Mr Edwards climbed aboard. Both women greeted him with welcoming smiles. He hesitated, and then took the seat beside Mrs Dankworth, who welcomed him warmly.

Etta saw from the glances that passed between other passengers that this little episode had been noted.

'Do many tourists come back?' Etta asked quietly as Kaan took his seat beside her.

'Quite a few. They realise how much there is to see and enjoy in Istanbul alone.'

'And do you like Istanbul?'

'Of course. It's my home.'

She laughed. 'Do you know, I'd forgotten you must have a home somewhere? I had somehow imagined you as always in a coach, constantly travelling from one sight to the next.'

'I have a home, and a family, as I told you.' He turned to her. 'I've been meaning to talk about that. You do know you don't have to go home as soon as the tour is over, don't you? Harry was going to stay for at least another week. Why don't you do that, too? I could show you Istanbul properly, and you might even meet my family.'

He was prepared to introduce her to his family? That was definitely an offer of friendship, but she was a little wary.

'How would they feel about a stranger suddenly appearing in their midst? It sounds as if your mother has enough to cope with already with your family.'

He grinned. 'Etta, my mother never has any difficulty in coping with anything. I've met your mother — briefly — and spoken to her on the phone. Obviously she is a formidable woman, but I can assure you that she would meet her match in my mother.'

His voice was warm. He might have a healthy respect for his mother, but he was obviously very fond of her as well.

'In that case, I'm not sure I should meet her. My own mother is quite enough for me,' was Etta's reply.

'I think you would find her very interesting. You'd appreciate the contrast with your mother — and the similarities.'

165

'I'm very grateful for your offer and I will think about it.'

The more she thought about it, the more attractive the idea became, but Etta decided she should wait until she heard what her mother had to say that evening before making up her mind what to do during the next few days. After all, her mother might still need her support, though it seemed unlikely after last night's phone call.

* * *

The coach drove on smoothly until they stopped for lunch at a roadside restaurant, where Etta took the opportunity to speak to Burke and Hunt, wanting to check if their new friendliness had survived the night.

'Have you enjoyed the morning?' she asked brightly.

Burke gave her a bored look and did not bother to reply, but his friend managed a very unconvincing smile. 'I liked the scenery,' he acknowledged.

166

Etta thought that it was a big improvement, even if only one of the pair managed to be more sociable, but when she looked for them a few minutes later she realised that they had reverted to their old trick of vanishing as soon as they could. Then, once again, they reappeared just before departure time.

Etta reported this to Kaan, who nodded grimly. 'I know. I went looking for them and saw them talking to a stranger, so I went up to them and asked if they were lost and the man walked away quickly. They said they'd been asking him the way to the toilets, but as I'd already told everybody on the coach where they were, and since they were walking in the opposite direction, I didn't believe them.'

'But . . . ?'

'I don't know what they were talking about, but it's not an offence to talk to a stranger. All we know is that they are behaving a little oddly, so we go on watching them.'

'And David Trowbridge? What's his interest in them?'

'Once again, there's really nothing wrong with that, and why should you care anyway?'

She had no answer ready and his voice became impatient. 'Etta, all we can do is watch and wait. Personally I hope that the three of them finish the tour in Istanbul without anything dramatic happening, then fly away, and we never see them again. After all, I don't want Top Turkish Tours getting involved in anything that's going to mean bad publicity.'

There was silence after that until Etta began to shift uneasily. 'I know these are very comfortable seats, but I do get tired of sitting still,' she complained. 'How do you put up with it week after week?'

'I don't tour every week,' he replied. 'I spend quite a lot of my time in Istanbul.'

'Oh, what do you do?'

'This and that,' he said evasively, and

was obviously not prepared to say more. She was hurt. He had invited her to meet his family, but now he was shutting her out again.

They were approaching Istanbul and Etta was deep in thought, wondering what dinner that night would reveal about the situation between her mother and George Trent, and what she could find to wear from her suitcase that would meet with her mother's approval.

Kaan looked at his watch and stood up, ready to address the tourists. He had just started to explain what they would be seeing the next day when suddenly there was a scream of brakes and a crash of metal on metal. In front of them a car had tried to cut into an outer lane but the space had proved too small, and another car had run into it.

The coach driver had frantically slammed on his brakes, but the coach could not stop instantly and, for an awful second, Etta had a mental picture of the coach full of travellers hitting the two cars. The coach wheels slid along the road surface, then gripped, and the coach stopped inches from the crashed cars.

Kaan, taken by surprise, was flung sideways, lost his footing and fell, hitting his head on the metal handrail on a seat back. He lay still, crumpled on the floor. As the tourists either screamed or stood up, craning to see what was happening, Etta flung herself down beside Kaan, taking him in her arms, her heart thudding madly.

There was blood on his face and his eyes were closed. 'Kaan, Kaan! Wake up!' she begged him.

She gasped with relief as his eyes opened after a few seconds and he blinked at her dazedly, struggling to sit up.

'Are you all right?' Etta demanded.

'I think so ... ' Weakly, with no regard for his own situation, he pointed urgently at the passengers. 'Etta! Get them all to sit down, now!'

Obediently Etta stood up and turned to face the anxious coach-load, speaking as firmly and loudly as she could.

'Kaan's all right, but all of you, please, sit down at once. We don't want any more accidents.'

Thankfully, they all obeyed, and with her help and that of the coach-driver Kaan managed to pull himself up and sink into his seat just as the wail of a police siren was heard. Etta located the first-aid box and wiped away the blood from a deep cut on his forehead before she found a large plaster to cover the wound. Soon the police were ordering them to drive on past the two crashed cars and they were once more on the way to Istanbul.

'Are you sure you are all right?' Etta said once more to Kaan. He looked very white and blood was seeping through the plaster.

He managed a travesty of a smile. 'I've felt better, but I'll survive, though I expect I'll have the worst headache of my life in a bit.' He winced. 'And I can feel some nasty bruises developing already.'

'I'm not leaving the group tonight.

You're in no state to cope. In fact, you're going to bed as soon as we reach the hotel,' Etta said decisively.

He started to shake his head, but that was obviously too painful and he stopped and groaned. 'I can manage.'

'I doubt if you can stand up without falling over. I'm staying with you, so don't bother to argue.'

He managed a feeble grin but there was genuine gratitude in his eyes. 'In that case, thank you very much, and you can tell your mother it's all my fault.'

They reached the Istanbul hotel without any further incident.

Etta helped Kaan to sit down in the lounge while she busied herself at Reception until all the guests had gone up to their rooms. When she went to find him again he was sunk in an armchair, his eyes closed, lines of pain marking his face.

Her lips tightened and she leaned forward and shook his arm gently. He opened his eyes and looked up at her, but seemed to have difficulty in focussing.

'That settles it. You're going to a hospital to get checked out,' she told him firmly.

'Actually, I think that might be a good idea,' he admitted and his compliance made her suddenly afraid. He must be feeling ill!

The coach was still outside the hotel, as the driver had just finished unloading the luggage. He nodded wordlessly when Etta told him what she wanted done, then came into the hotel and the two of them supported Kaan as far as the coach.

She stood looking after it anxiously as it drew away, then squared her shoulders and re-entered the hotel. Now she was in sole charge of thirty tourists!

An hour later she learned in a phone call from Kaan that her responsibility was going to last for longer than she had anticipated.

'The hospital wants to keep me in

overnight,' he said gloomily. 'They think I might have concussion. Will you phone the company and ask them to send someone to replace me tomorrow morning? I know you're a quick learner and I can rely on you to deal with anything to do with the hotel, but the Istanbul tour really needs someone who knows the city well.'

'Don't worry.' She tried to sound confident. 'I can cope.'

'Etta, I trust you, but you'll need a guide for the tour.'

After the call had ended she rang Top Turkish Tours' number and explained the situation to the man who answered.

He was obviously upset to hear about Kaan's accident, made her promise to call again if there was any new developments, and told her that another guide familiar with Istanbul would be at the hotel early in the morning. He finished by assuring her that if she needed any more help she only had to call him, which made her feel much better.

Next she called her mother's mobile

number. There was no answer, but she left a message, briefly explaining the situation, and feeling quite pleased that she did not have to experience her mother's reaction directly.

Then, having checked with the hotel that the tourists could either dine in the hotel or at a nearby restaurant if they preferred, she decided she had earned a short break and sat down to relax for the first time that day.

6

Most of the tourists had decided on dinner in the hotel, but among the more adventurous souls Etta saw Burke and Hunt making for the door. Geoff Hunt still had his shoulder bag slung across him and Etta smiled at him, pointing to the bag as they passed her on their way out. 'You could leave your bag in your room safe,' she suggested.

He looked startled, then clutched his bag as if afraid she would take it from him forcibly and shook his head. 'I've heard stories,' he said darkly. 'I prefer to keep it with me.'

Soon after they had left David Trowbridge appeared, also apparently ready to look for a restaurant.

'Your friends have just left,' Etta told him. He lifted an eyebrow. 'Mr Burke and Mr Hunt.'

She watched to see if there was any

reaction, and saw his lips tighten slightly, but then he shrugged and laughed.

'I wouldn't call them my friends, but thanks for the warning. Tell me which way they went and I'll go in the other direction. I don't want to be stuck with those two.'

The lobby was emptying and Etta guessed there would be no call on her services until after everyone had eaten. No doubt by then someone would inevitably have found some cause for complaint. Some guests seemed to compete to see who could find the most faults in their rooms. At least Mrs Dankworth had not been so ready to complain since she had become friendly with Mr Edwards.

It seemed a good opportunity to have something to eat herself, but as she moved towards the dining room there was a familiar click of high heels on the tiled floor and her mother's imperious voice stopped her in her tracks.

'Etta!'

She turned as her mother swept towards her and saw that the older woman was indeed once again her usual self; her dress obviously from a famous designer, her accessories carefully matched, and her hair and make-up immaculate.

'I gathered from your message that for some strange reason you can't come to the Club this evening, so — although it was very inconvenient — I have changed all my arrangements and come to see you. I want to talk to you.'

'If you must, Mother, but can we talk over dinner? I'm absolutely starving.'

Mrs Trent looked dubiously round the hotel lobby and shuddered but then steeled herself.

'Why not? I suppose people do have to eat here.'

Etta cringed as she saw various indignant hotel staff within earshot glare at her mother.

In the dining room Mrs Trent carefully inspected the cutlery, reorganised the table setting, quizzed the waiter about the available wines, and was obviously taken aback when she found she had to get her own food from the buffet. However, having tasted her carefully-chosen starter, she grudgingly announced that it was actually quite edible.

Etta relaxed. She explained about Kaan's accident and his overnight stay in the hospital. Her mother reluctantly accepted that this was an adequate explanation, while Etta, who had had a very early breakfast and a light lunch and was feeling really hungry, ate in silence for several minutes until she looked up and caught her mother's impatient look.

'Okay,' she said, laying down her knife and fork. 'I am really longing to know what happened between the time when you left me as an utter wreck and your marvellous recovery. What do you want to tell me?'

Her mother actually giggled. Etta, who had never heard this sound from her mother's lips before, looked at her sharply, but Mrs Trent was carefully avoiding her eyes.

'George and I had a long talk last night,' she said, tracing circles on the tabletop with her finger. 'Mostly we talked about the two of us . . . '

She finally looked up, her eyes full of wonder. 'Do you know, all the time I was scheming to attract him, to get him to marry me, he knew what I was doing and let me go ahead because he wanted me. He wanted me!'

She shook her head, as if she could hardly believe what she had just said. 'All my life I seem to have been plotting and scheming to get what I wanted, persuading people to fall in with my plans, and then the man I wanted most, the big prize, actually wanted me!

'I was so happy when he told me. Apparently he didn't tell me before because he thought the only person I had ever really loved was your father. Yesterday, when he realised how I really felt about Henry, he decided to be frank about his feelings. We talked for ages, but the upshot was that we realised that we really do care for each other — deeply.'

'I'm so glad!' Etta said, warmly and genuinely.

Secretly she marvelled at the realisation that her mother had suffered from insecurity and lack of belief in herself. Perhaps it had been due to her rejection by her first love, Etta's father. She had certainly never let a hint of it appear — but perhaps her domineering behaviour had been an attempt to compensate for her secret lack of confidence.

'Isn't it marvellous?' her mother continued, but then a trace of the old steely glare appeared. 'We did talk about you as well. George says that it's time I let you go properly, that you're old enough to decide what you want to do for yourself, and that of course you will make mistakes but you'll learn from them.'

She examined Etta critically, and shrugged as if puzzled. 'He said you are very like me, so I shouldn't worry about you.'

Both women were silent for a moment, both wondering whether George was right.

'Anyway,' Mrs Trent said, 'I agreed I'd try not to interfere — to guide you — too much in the future. Though I'll always be ready to help if you need me, and I'm not going to cut off your allowance,' she added hastily. 'After all, there's no reason why I shouldn't give you good advice when you need it.'

Etta braced herself. Old habits were definitely going to die hard and her mother would have extreme difficulty in restraining herself from telling her only child what to do. 'For example, this message you left about the travel rep leaving you alone and in charge . . . he knows you are inexperienced. Even if he did have concussion he should have insisted that the travel firm send someone else to take over.'

'Well, he did try to actually,' Etta replied defensively. 'I was the one who insisted and I was glad he felt that he could leave me in charge. It shows he trusts me, that he thinks I've learned a lot over the past few days.'

Her mother was looking at her thoughtfully. 'You are very eager to defend this young man.'

'Kaan has been very good to me.'

'You've only known him a few days.'

'Long enough to know how kind he is.'

'I see . . . and is he perhaps aware that you come from a wealthy background?'

Recalling her conversations with Kaan, Etta didn't reply, but her mother could read the answer in her face.

'Oh, dear. I might as well tell you that I saw Miles Standing a couple of evenings ago,' Mrs Trent confessed. 'I ignored him at first, but he came up and insisted on speaking to me. He said he wanted to warn me that he thought this Kaan might be taking advantage of you. Of course, I don't trust him an inch after what we found out about him, but now I'm wondering if he might have been right for once.'

Etta's cheeks were red with fury as she cried out, 'That nasty, lying worm! I refused to let him carry me off back to you, then he almost tried to kidnap me, so he was just trying to get his own back!'

Rapidly she told her mother of Standing's recent appearance and how he had been rejected, but before her mother could give her reaction to this, the hotel receptionist hurried up to Etta.

'Miss Sanderson, there's a lady at Reception. She's asking for Mr Talbot, so I thought you could explain what's happened to him and why he's not here.'

'Of course.' Etta stood up, smiling apologetically at her mother. 'I'll just deal with this, then I'll be right back.'

Probably it was someone from the travel firm, she guessed as she followed the girl . . . or it could be a girlfriend? What would she say then?

As it turned out it was neither. The lady waiting impatiently by the desk was probably nearing fifty and comfortably built, but still very attractive. Her long robe of purple silk blended eastern and western dress, and no travel rep would have had quite so much heavy gold jewellery displayed at her neck. When Etta appeared she looked at her with surprise and raised her perfect arched eyebrows a fraction of an inch.

'You wanted to see Mr Talbot?' Etta enquired.

'I have already told the girl that,' the woman said impatiently in perfect unaccented English, giving an icy glare at the receptionist, who was trying to hide behind the desk.

'I'm afraid he's not available tonight,' Etta replied politely. 'But I am sure I can help you . . . '

'Where is he?' The woman's impatient voice cut across Etta's little speech.

'I'm afraid he's in hospital.'

The woman's eyes widened and she

seemed to stop breathing. 'In hospital?'

'Yes, so can I help?' Etta offered a little desperately.

'Kaan is my son! What has happened to him? Which hospital? I must know!'

Etta gasped, then realised that the golden eyes glaring at her were identical to Kaan's. 'Mrs Talbot! Was Kaan expecting you?'

'*Where is he?*'

This time the enquiry was almost shouted.

Etta decided to settle for the bare facts. 'Very near here. The coach driver braked suddenly and Kaan fell and hit his head: He's fine really, but the hospital was worried about concussion so they decided to keep him overnight just to make quite sure he is all right.'

Mrs Talbot's hands tightened into fists. 'If he has had to stay in the hospital, he must be hurt.'

'Kaan did hurt his head but really, he's not badly injured. Keeping him overnight is just a precaution. You don't need to worry about him,' Etta said hurriedly.

'It was the driver's fault? I will speak to him!'

'If he hadn't braked the coach would have crashed into two cars and people would have been killed,' Etta explained.

Mrs Talbot thought about this and was forced to accept the explanation, her anger fading gradually, but then she frowned. 'And who are you? What about the tour and the guests?'

Etta was not sure what this had to do with Mrs Talbot, unless she was worried about the effect on Kaan, but rapidly explained her situation anyway. It did not seem to reassure Mrs Talbot.

'So, you are inexperienced as a tour guide and you have never been to Istanbul before?'

'The travel company is sending an experienced guide in the morning,' Etta said quickly.

Mrs Talbot nodded slowly and reluctantly. 'Then please tell me the name of the hospital where Kaan was taken so I can go there immediately.'

The information was given, and Mrs Talbot turned on her heel in a swish of silk and strode towards the door.

Etta followed and saw that the space outside the hotel was dominated by two large limousines, each with a uniformed chauffeur. Etta recognised one as that belonging to George and her mother. The other chauffeur leapt out of the car as Mrs Talbot approached, opened the rear door and carefully saw her seated, before driving off.

Etta's mother was looking very thoughtful by the time her daughter returned to her cold coffee.

'I followed you and I was listening to all that,' she said before Etta had even sat down. 'I very nearly told her that my daughter was perfectly capable of dealing with the situation.'

Etta was suddenly struck by the fact that Kaan had been right, that her mother and Mrs Talbot were very alike in some ways. Her mother was dressed in the latest Paris fashion and careful diet and exercise had kept her slender, as opposed to the flowing robes and full figure of Mrs Talbot. But both were elegant, carefully groomed women, and both clearly had very strong personalities.

She recalled Kaan's comments on his mother.

'Not many travel reps have mothers who can afford chauffeur-driven limousines,' Mrs Trent was commenting. 'And did you see her jewellery? Not my style, but extremely expensive. What do you know about this Kaan you are working with?'

'I know he's a good guide and rep, but I know very little about his family,' Etta confessed. 'Except that his father was English and his mother is Turkish.'

'Do try and find out. It might be interesting,' she said with a wry smile. 'Oh, and I agree with you about Miles Standing. I'll spread the word among our friends in case he tries any more of his tricks.'

The smile was gone and Mrs Trent

reverted to her more usual efficient tone. 'Now, the main reason I wanted to see you today was to find out what you want to do when this little tour of yours is over. Do you want to stay in Istanbul, fly back to England, or come on the yacht with us?'

So it was decision time. Etta had ruled out flying back to England, and she was afraid that Kaan's offer of family hospitality might have been an impulse which he had since regretted, even before his accident.

'I would like to come on the yacht, actually,' she announced. 'I think it's just what I need after the past few days.'

Etta was amazed to see her mother's face light up. 'Oh, I'm so glad! We'll have a wonderful time!'

Before either of them could say any more a middle-aged woman loomed over their table.

'The cold tap in my bathroom is dripping,' she complained without any preliminaries. 'Will you please have it fixed before it keeps me awake all night?'

'Of course,' Etta said smoothly, rising to her feet. 'Mother, it looks as if I am going to be busy. I'll call you soon.'

Mrs Talbot blinked, opened her mouth to speak, but then saw Etta's firm expression, and reluctantly accepted her dismissal.

Etta had the tap dealt with, as well as a couple of other minor complaints which had arisen. She then seized the opportunity to phone the hospital and was reassured that Kaan had not developed any alarming symptoms.

Tired and grateful, she finally went to bed.

★　★　★

When the alarm woke her in the morning, Etta started the day in a happy mood. Kaan would probably be back later that morning, and although she had coped adequately so far she would feel much better when he was back to guide her.

She felt even better when she discovered that a message from the travel firm was waiting for her at the desk when she went down to breakfast, confirming that a guide familiar with Istanbul would be there before the coach left, so Etta would be able to relax and enjoy the tour of the fabulous ancient city of Istanbul and its treasures.

Not only that, but she was now happily aware that her mother had apparently at long last accepted that her daughter was now a responsible and capable adult!

What could go wrong?

Breakfast went smoothly, the coach arrived at the hotel in plenty of time, and Etta waited for the new guide to arrive . . .

And waited. And waited.

The tour was supposed to start at nine o'clock, and the tourists were already assembled by ten minutes to the hour, eager to see the splendours of Istanbul.

Etta wondered what had gone wrong. Had the guide gone to the wrong hotel? Had a vital message gone astray?

Then, at one minute to nine, the door opened and a figure strolled in very casually, saw the assembled party, smiled, and waved a greeting before leisurely joining them.

'Hello. Top Turkish Tours? I'm your guide for today.'

No one said anything in reply. They were all just standing and staring at the beautiful newcomer.

She was probably in her mid-twenties and had shoulder-length shining blonde hair, big brown eyes, and her brows and incredibly long eyelashes were dark against her lightly-tanned skin. The silence did not seem to upset her; she was probably used to this reaction.

She looked round. 'Where's Kaan?' she said with a touch of impatience. 'I understood he would be here. He is in charge of this party, isn't he?'

Etta cleared her throat. 'I'm afraid Kaan's not here. I'm Etta Sanderson and I'm in charge of the group today.'

The blonde's smile vanished and her eyes went icy cold. For a moment Etta thought the new guide was about to turn on her heel and leave, but instead she frowned enquiringly. 'Why are you here and not Kaan?'

'Kaan has had a minor accident,' Etta explained, 'but he should be back with us later today.'

'An accident? What kind of an accident?' There was an echo of his mother's voice here.

'Nothing serious.' Etta explained what had happened on the coach and was rewarded with a satisfied smile.

'So I will see him later.' The blonde looked round at the waiting tourists. 'The coach is waiting. Shall we start?'

They followed her outside obediently, though Etta did hear Mrs Dankworth muttering to Mr Edwards that anybody would have thought the tourists had kept her waiting instead of the other way around. For the first time, Etta thought that Mrs Dankworth definitely had her good points.

Etta had a growing suspicion, confirmed when she followed the last passenger on to the coach, took her seat by the new guide and was casually informed, 'I'm Allegra, by the way.'

So this was the woman who had rejected Kaan!

But the following hours proved that at least Allegra was a very efficient and knowledgeable guide to the glories of Istanbul. She guided them competently through the Roman Hippodrome, showed them the splendours of the Blue Mosque and the imposing Hagia Sophia.

She was crisply informative and ready to answer questions from the tourists, and although as the morning grew hotter the members of the groups began to sweat and wilt, Allegra stayed fresh and cool. She virtually ignored Etta unless there was some minor errand to be undertaken, such as rounding up straggling tourists.

When they had a mid-morning break she sent Etta to fetch her a cup of coffee and then indicated that Etta should sit beside her. The interrogation began.

'You don't work for our firm,' Allegra remarked. 'So how is it that you are with Kaan on this tour?'

'My firm in England sent me here to see what the tours are really like, and to get some hands-on experience.'

Allegra raised an eyebrow. 'And how have you got on?'

'I think I've done quite well,' Etta said defensively. 'Kaan seems to think so, anyway.'

Allegra carefully put down her coffee cup. 'So you have got on well with Kaan?'

'He has been very kind and helpful.' Etta couldn't help the defensive tone of her voice.

Allegra gave a brittle laugh. 'Oh, I'm sure he has been. He always tries to help the little lame ducks.'

She looked Etta over, very slowly and very critically. 'I suppose with a little more experience you wouldn't end the tour looking quite so crumpled. And you really should have your hair cut shorter; it would be easier to manage.'

Without giving Etta a chance to reply, she stood up and clapped her hands, indicating that it was time to get back on the coach.

As Etta sat beside Allegra in the coach she was seething, and decided that she had probably never disliked anybody so thoroughly or so instantly in her life. It didn't help that she seemed to be the only one to feel like this. The men on the trip were eyeing Allegra with open admiration, and some of the women seemed to be almost awestruck.

'She's so efficient — and so glamorous!' Mary West whispered dreamily to her, apparently realising seconds later that this was not altogether a tactful statement. 'Of course, she has had more experience than you,' she added hastily, and returned to her fiancé's side.

Etta was left brooding darkly.

* * *

Lunch was followed by a restful cruise up the Bosphorus, gazing at the palaces and splendid villas that lined its shores. Allegra somehow managed to suggest that she was a close friend of most of the owners of these beautiful residences. The cool breeze that blew in off the sea was most welcome after the heat of the city, and most of the passengers relaxed on sun loungers, happy to let the impressive scenery simply roll past before their eyes.

Then the coach was waiting to return them to the hotel.

Etta was eagerly looking forward to this. She wanted to get away from Allegra to her own room so that she could think about the possible significance of the girl's unexpected reappearance.

As the tourists descended from the bus and Etta turned to follow them into the hotel, Allegra placed a firm, delaying hand on her arm. 'As you could see today, my dear,' she purred, 'you are not really needed on the tour. I can manage on my own tomorrow — or with Kaan, if he has recovered.'

'I don't mind coming,' Etta said stiffly. 'Tomorrow we're going to the Topkapi Palace. I don't want to miss that — and I do want to see more of Istanbul, as well as learning how to lead a tour.'

Allegra shrugged. 'Really, you'll just be in the way — but I suppose it will up to Kaan to decide.'

As they went in the door of the hotel they could hear sudden exclamations and a babble of comments from the clients. The reason was soon obvious. Kaan stood in the centre of the reception area, smiling and looking in perfect health, with only a large square of sticking plaster on his forehead to show what had happened the previous day.

'Kaan!' Allegra exclaimed immediately, then suddenly thrust herself through the tourists who were congratulating Kaan and flung her arms around him. 'I was so worried about you!'

Kaan's arms went round Allegra, although Etta, watching the scene through narrowed eyes, decided that he was only trying to avoid being knocked over and that he looked more bewildered than delighted.

'Allegra! What are you doing here?' he demanded, disentangling himself. He was holding the beautiful blonde's hands, though it was impossible to tell whether it was out of affection or to prevent her seizing him again.

'Didn't the office tell you? As soon as I heard about your awful accident I insisted on coming to take over the tour. I've been worrying about you all day and I'm so glad to see you have recovered.'

She's lying, Etta thought indignantly. Allegra hadn't even known about Kaan's accident until she had arrived at the hotel and Etta had told her.

Allegra stood close to Kaan, gazing into his eyes. Etta gave a swift glance at the fascinated audience of tourists and decided he should be rescued, whether he wanted to be or not.

She stepped forward briskly. 'We've all been worried, Kaan, and we're glad to see you back safe and well,' she said breezily. 'Allegra has been a tremendous help today, but she can relax now that the two of us are back in charge.' She smiled.

Allegra's face was still set in a smile, but she was looking daggers at Etta as she retorted, 'I think you still need me. Your . . . helper knows nothing about Istanbul.'

'Maybe you can help us tomorrow,' Kaan told her firmly. 'Although it depends on what the office says, of course. But you've done enough for today and I'm very grateful for that, and now you can go home and rest. Etta and I will take over for the rest of the day.'

Allegra hesitated, frowning, then decided to give in gracefully. 'Now I've seen you are safe and well I can go, but

I'll be here in the morning. Goodnight, Kaan. Don't overdo things . . . let little Etta do what she can.'

Then, with a flashing smile and a swirl of skirts and hair she was gone. The show over, the tourists began to drift away to their rooms to get ready for dinner.

Kaan gave Etta a wry smile. 'So you have met Allegra!'

'I've spent the whole day with her,' Etta said tersely.

'In that case you most definitely deserve a drink. Let me buy you one.'

7

Both of them sank gratefully into the welcoming armchairs. Kaan lay back and closed his eyes and Etta took the opportunity to study him carefully.

His tan prevented him from looking too pale, but he definitely had less colour than usual, his pallor contrasting with the dark crescent of his eyelashes against his cheeks and against the silky darkness of his hair. A few wisps had fallen across his forehead; instinctively she leaned forward and carefully moved them aside with one finger.

As she did so, he opened his eyes suddenly and for a moment they looked at each other intently before he gave his familiar twisted grin and tried to sit upright.

'You didn't have to come back today,' she told him reproachfully. 'I was coping with the usual little problems very well, you know.'

The waiter arrived with two tall, cool glasses and Kaan took a deep gulp from his before replying.

'Don't worry about me. I'm all right, really. I just had an awful headache and of course I didn't sleep much last night. Nurses kept checking to see if I was all right.

'I suppose I was worrying about the tour as well,' he confessed. 'I knew I didn't have to worry about you, but I didn't know who the company would send to take you round the city.'

'Allegra was a good guide to Istanbul,' she said, but did not elaborate further. Instead she looked at him, not quite able to bring herself to ask the question she really wanted to ask.

He shook his head. 'No, I really didn't know it would be Allegra. In fact it never occurred to me. I wasn't even sure she was still working with us.'

'Were you glad to see her?' she could not resist asking.

He fidgeted with his glass, not

meeting her eyes. 'It was a shock to see her, to tell you the truth. But in a way, as the man in charge of the tour, I was relieved because I knew she would have done a good job as a guide.

'As for how I felt personally, it may sound stupid but I really don't know, and I certainly didn't expect her to greet me as warmly as she did.'

'She is very beautiful,' Etta said awkwardly.

'She is indeed.' He said that perhaps a little too readily before he paused. 'But let's forget about her for the moment. Have there been any interesting incidents with our clients? And what did you think of Istanbul?'

'Someone had a dripping tap . . . I got that fixed. Mrs Dankworth and Mr Edwards seem to be getting closer, much to everyone's amusement, and Mrs Pritchard is being a good loser . . . Istanbul . . . well, Istanbul is simply marvellous!'

'Which bits did you like best?'

'The Blue Mosque, of course, but

there were lots of other things,' Etta enthused. 'I liked the monument made from captured Persian spears. It was such a good way of proclaiming their triumph. And I'd really like one of the luxury villas on the Bosphorus but I'm not sure that even George could afford that!'

Her enthusiasm was genuine, but nevertheless she had a sneaky feeling that she was being skilfully sidetracked with Kaan's talk of Istanbul.

'What did your mother say when she found you in hospital?' Etta asked abruptly, interrupting a eulogy on Hagia Sophia.

Kaan blinked. 'How do you know she came to see me?' he said with surprise.

'She came here first and I had to tell her what had happened and where you were.'

'Oh. She didn't say how she knew I was there. I thought someone from the office might have contacted her.'

His look reminded Etta of a naughty schoolboy. 'After she was reassured

— at length — that I was not badly hurt, she spent her time trying to reorganise the hospital so that all its resources would be dedicated to me. Finally one of the doctors politely asked her to leave. He said I needed quiet — and so did the rest of the hospital after her visit!'

'Yes, she did seem a rather formidable woman . . . ' Etta said very carefully.

'She is! Fortunately she's always on my side against the rest of the world, no matter how critical of me she may be in private.'

That was clearly all he was prepared to say about his mother, changing the subject abruptly back to the tourists.

'Most of them will be going home tomorrow, of course,' he said. 'But as you know there are the few who have booked a three-day extension in Istanbul, and although we don't take them out we are still responsible for looking after them generally.'

He named those who would be

staying; there were about a dozen and they included an Australian couple and two English couples. 'Mr David Trowbridge is staying on, too,' Kaan added. 'Which will probably please you, and — and this might surprise you — Burke and Hunt.'

'Those two? But they were bored stiff even in Istanbul! I thought they were going to fall asleep from sheer boredom.'

'Nevertheless, they're spending three more days here. I wonder what they'll do? At least we won't have to try to find something they'll enjoy.'

Half an hour passed in discussion of the day and the departure of clients the following day, and they found they had very little time to rush upstairs to change for dinner.

As usual, they were seated some distance away from their clients, but they were aware of more noise and laughter than usual, and that the waiters were bringing out more bottles of wine than on previous evenings.

'Last night of the holiday,' Kaan commented. 'If it's been a good trip it usually turns into an informal party. I expect we'll be invited over — that's always a good sign that the tour has been a success.'

It was in fact Mr Edwards who approached them ten minutes later. 'We're having a little get-together in the bar after dinner,' he informed them. 'Just to celebrate a most enjoyable holiday. We'll all be very pleased if you'll join us.'

With the exception of Burke and Hunt, everybody gathered in the bar. There was still one excursion left, because the next morning they were to visit the Topkapi Palace before returning to the hotel to collect their luggage and go on to the airport. But this was their last real opportunity to relax and chat together.

Addresses were being exchanged, invitations recklessly offered, and many promises being made to email the best photographs. Toasts were proposed,

Etta and Kaan were thanked, and Mr Edwards asked Kaan to pass their thanks on to the driver as well.

Kaan made an amusing little speech in return, which he quietly admitted to Etta he had made many times before.

Etta noticed that Mrs Dankworth and Mr Edwards sat close together, as if determined to enjoy each other's company for these last few hours.

Valerie Pritchard found an opportunity for a few words. 'Look at my two friends,' she murmured, nodding at Mrs Dankworth and Mr Edwards. 'I think this holiday might be the start of something big for the two of them.'

She giggled. 'I thought I was going to commandeer him. I must be losing my touch! But I don't mind. I think they'll be happy, and I'm very glad.'

Etta realised as she finally made her way up to her room that she would miss all the tourists — even those she had disliked. This had been her first experience as a tour rep and she knew she would remember it vividly, even if future tours were less memorable.

Her first tour? She was thinking of coming on more?

★ ★ ★

The morning excursion started a little later than usual the next day, which gave those who were leaving time to pack and others time to recover from the night before.

Allegra appeared precisely on time, looking just as beautiful as the day before. She told Kaan he looked in perfect health and handsomer than ever, but stared coldly at Etta, who was standing quietly beside him.

'As I said yesterday, there's no need for you to come with us, Miss Sanderson,' she purred. 'Kaan and I will be perfectly all right without you.'

'Etta is coming as my guest, not as a rep,' Kaan interposed swiftly. 'I want to show her the Topkapi Palace.'

'Just so long as she doesn't get in the way,' Allegra muttered ungraciously, and proceeded to ignore Etta's existence.

However, for most of the morning Etta could not have cared less about Allegra's unwelcoming behaviour. She was entranced by the splendour and beauty of the Topkapi Palace. The golden thrones and jewelled daggers gave some idea of the wealth of the former Turkish rulers, but also conveyed their power and made Etta understand for the first time why the Turks had been such a threat to the rulers of Europe.

But Etta could not remain completely unaware of the way Allegra stayed close to Kaan, occasionally appealing to him for more information, then thanking him warmly for his help. There was a possessive air about her attitude towards him which stirred feelings that Etta diagnosed as anger. Because it couldn't possibly be jealousy, could it?

She told herself not to be stupid. She and Kaan had worked amicably enough together for a few days, but that was all. Theirs was a brief working relationship and after a few days, she would probably never see him again. If he preferred the beautiful Allegra — and Etta knew how badly he had wanted her at one time — then it was none of her business.

But the feelings refused to go away. Kaan was attractive, intelligent, understanding — natural that Etta, dependent upon him for guidance, felt gratitude that might be mistaken for a warmer emotion. At least, that was what she told herself.

The tour was definitely ending on a high note with all the tourists spellbound by this final spectacle. Even Burke and Hunt were to be seen examining an enormous emerald with real interest. Surprisingly, it was David Trowbridge who seemed uninterested, giving the famous exhibits only a brief glance.

When Etta lightly challenged him over this, he simply shrugged. 'They're all very nice, but useless shut away behind all these security devices. You need to touch things of beauty to enjoy them properly.'

He gave her a long, meaningful glance, and she found herself blushing. Turning away, she found Kaan watching the two of them, and her colour deepened.

It was nearly time to leave the Palace and return to the coach when Allegra, for once without Kaan, beckoned Etta.

'The Australian couple have wandered off over there,' she said, pointing to a corner of the building. 'Go and find them and bring them back to the coach.'

Etta was annoyed by being told so briskly to find the couple instead of being asked, but of course they could not risk abandoning the couple in the midst of the tourist crowds.

Obediently Etta set off on her errand, but no matter how hard she looked she could not see the missing pair. Glancing at her watch, she saw that it was time for the coach to leave. She had better tell Kaan of her failure to locate the couple and arrange for the coach to wait while she tried again.

But when she got to the car park she found the coach was gone! She stared around, desperately hoping that she had come to the wrong parking place, but there was no sign of the Top Tours vehicle. She knew Kaan would not have left until everyone was on board, including the Australian couple, so why had he left her? And what was she to do?

Feeling very lonely, she waited a quarter of an hour, hoping to see the coach reappear, but at the end of that time it was clear she would have to decide on a course of action. She would have to get back to the hotel, and the only way she could do that was by taking a taxi. Fortunately she had some money, and she was just starting to look for a taxi rank when a cab screeched to a halt beside her.

'You want taxi?' The driver was

already opening the door so she climbed in and gave him the name of the hotel.

'I know it.'

The taxi sped off and Etta relaxed — but not for long.

The driver seemed to be taking an unfamiliar route away from the central sights of Istanbul. Was he going to the wrong hotel? She tried to attract his attention but he waved a dismissive hand and drove on. It was quite a time before, to her relief, they drew up outside the right hotel.

'How much?' she asked, wondering about the tip, then almost dropped her purse as the driver told her how much he wanted. It was more than she had.

'That's far too much! And you took a long way round,' she accused him.

He repeated the amount, and she grew uncomfortably aware of how big he was, and how there was no one around to whom she could appeal.

Finally, desperately, she held her open purse out to him so he could see she could not pay the full extortionate fare. He took the purse, tipped all the money into the palm of his hand and then handed the empty purse back. She scrambled out of the taxi and ran to the hotel, almost in tears.

The coach arrived ten minutes later and Etta was waiting to challenge Kaan and Allegra. 'Why did you leave me at the Topkapi Palace?' she demanded.

Kaan looked at her with obvious surprise.

'Abandon you? But you told Allegra you wanted to stay there longer and would make your own way back.'

'I did not! Allegra told me a couple was missing so I went to look for them, and then I found the coach had gone without me.'

Allegra's expression was a mixture of puzzlement and concern. 'I said what?' She indicated the tourists. 'As you can see they are all here.'

'You said — '

'You must have misunderstood me,' Allegra said with finality.

Etta turned angrily to Kaan but he silenced her impatiently.

'Obviously there was some confusion,' he said. 'But you got back here all right, so all is well.'

Allegra turned to Kaan, placed a hand on his arm and smiled. 'I'll meet you at the restaurant, Kaan. I'm so looking forward to our evening together. I'll put on my prettiest dress.'

She walked away, not even deigning to look at Etta again.

So, Etta fumed, criticism of Allegra was not to be allowed. Kaan had been unfair, and it showed that the other guide was important to him.

But as the tourists who were leaving Istanbul that day picked up their luggage and a packed lunch and climbed back onto the coach for the last time, Kaan turned to Etta apologetically.

'I'm sorry I was so curt with you just now, but the truth is that I've got an awful headache and I just didn't feel up to refereeing an argument between the two of you.'

Etta instantly felt much better.

'Do you want to come to the airport?' she enquired.

'Yes. I've taken a couple of aspirins, so I should be all right.'

* * *

At the airport most of the holidaymakers remembered to thank the driver sincerely before heading for the check-in desks and their return to normal life.

Mary West and Gavin Preston went off happily together. Gavin had had his taste of the exotic unknown, and Mary could now return to planning her wedding. Etta was sure they suited each other well. Perhaps they would appear on touring holidays in the future, though she guessed they would more likely be found on beaches with their children, and she wished them well.

Unexpectedly Mrs Dankworth lingered for a final word. 'I have enjoyed myself,' she said almost defiantly. 'I know you think I fuss too much over little things, but a woman on her own has to look out for herself.'

She looked around almost furtively and added, 'Anyway . . . I may not be on my own much longer. Mr Edwards has asked if he can come and see me.' She giggled like a teenager. 'And he's made it quite plain he isn't thinking of one quick visit!'

'I'm very pleased — for both of you,' Etta said sincerely.

'And you're a very nice girl . . . ' Mrs Dankworth leaned closer. 'And Mr Talbot — Kaan — he's a very nice young man, as I'm sure you're aware.'

Etta smiled wryly. 'Didn't you notice today that he's got other interests, Mrs Dankworth?'

'Oh, you mean the blonde? She's got looks, of course, but there are definite hints of a nasty nature. He'll soon get tired of her. Well, goodbye, dear. Mr Edwards is waiting for me.'

Etta's opinion of Mrs Dankworth rose considerably.

As the last of the tourists moved out

of sight, she sighed with relief. This unexpected tour had been exhausting, but the hardest part was over. The remaining clients would wander round their favourite sights and museums for a few days by themselves, then they, too, would be brought to the airport and waved goodbye.

It had indeed been a tiring time and she was beginning to think a little wistfully of her own quiet flat and the familiar routine of work in England, almost regretting that she would not be on the plane that would be leaving for England in a couple of hours.

She would miss Kaan, of course, but in spite of Mrs Dankworth's encouraging words he had never shown any interest in her as anything but a fellow worker. And now the beautiful Allegra had apparently reawakened his interest.

'So what do we do now?' she asked him as they left the airport building.

'Well, after our coach has taken us back to our hotel we have a few free hours to do anything we want. In my case, I think it means nothing more exciting than catching up with laundry and paperwork and then having a rest. What about you?'

'Much the same, but tomorrow I'd like to go back to some of the places in Istanbul by myself and get to know the city well.'

'You'll need more than a day for that,' he warned her, ushering her towards the waiting coach, his arm casually around her shoulders. 'I've lived in Istanbul for a long time, and I'm still discovering new things about it. But in the next few days I can show you things that tourists usually miss.'

She opened her mouth to tell him that she wouldn't be staying in Istanbul, that she had agreed to go on the yacht with her mother, but decided to break the news later.

'Anyway,' he was saying, 'it sounds as if you have enjoyed your work experience, even if we did get off to a bad start — for which I apologise, incidentally.'

222

'I can understand you being annoyed when you got me instead of Harry,' she said. 'And you have been very kind and helpful since.'

His smile grew wider. 'It's easy to be kind and helpful to such a pretty girl.'

★   ★   ★

Their plans for a quiet afternoon were to be disrupted. Outside the hotel a highly-polished limousine was parked, whose chauffeur greeted Kaan with a smile.

'Mrs Talbot is inside waiting for you, sir. She has been waiting some time . . .'

There was a definite note of warning and Kaan grimaced, shrugged his shoulders.

'Thank you.' He turned to Etta. 'Unfortunately my mother still tends to regard me as a little boy in need of protection and seeing me in the hospital definitely upset her.

'Why don't you come with me, Etta, so you can reassure her that I have not been collapsing all over the airport?'

When they entered the hotel foyer they saw the receptionist's face light up with unmistakable relief.

'Mr Talbot! Your mother . . . '

'I know. Is she in the lounge?'

The receptionist nodded and Kaan strode through into the lounge, followed by Etta.

Mrs Talbot, dressed in flowing blue this morning, was sitting bolt upright on a couch, an untouched cup of coffee on the table in front of her. When she saw her son approaching she leapt to her feet and enveloped him in a generous embrace, while Etta stood near enough to hear the conversation between mother and son without being too intrusive.

Mrs Talbot was not happy.

'Kaan! You have been injured and I told you to rest! I came to take you home with me but instead I was told that you were out with the coach, carrying on as if nothing was the matter!'

Kaan gently detached himself and led his mother back to the couch. 'Because nothing *is* the matter with me, Mother. I had a slight bump on the head, a little scratch, but now I am perfectly all right. Miss Sanderson can confirm that if you ask her.'

He indicated Etta, but Mrs Talbot barely spared her a glance and a quick nod. Her comments were all too audible, however.

'Oh, yes. You mean the girl I met the other evening who told me what had happened to you. I still don't understand why she is here. She has had no tour experience, according to Allegra.'

'She is here to learn and to see how we look after our clients,' Kaan broke in. 'Mother, you may not know it, but Etta was kind enough to come here to accompany the tour at very short notice. Not only that, but she has learned a great deal very quickly. I shall certainly give her a very good report.'

Etta glowed with pleasure at this tribute.

But his mother's carefully plucked eyebrows lifted a quarter of an inch. 'Well! I don't think Allegra would agree with you. She came back to the office after your tour and I was talking to her before I came here. She told me that Miss Sanderson was of very little use at all.'

Etta's pleasure vanished as a red tide of anger rose up her neck and on to her face.

'Perhaps that was because she wouldn't let her do anything!' Kaan said quickly, and then bowed his head in his hands. 'At this rate I will have another very bad headache soon! Mother, listen to me, please.'

His mother opened her mouth to speak, looked at her son's face, and fell silent.

'First of all,' he said carefully, 'I would like you to know that when I was injured it was Etta who cared for me and gave me first aid, and who made sure that the tourists were safe. Secondly, why did the company send

Allegra to take the tour yesterday? She is not one of our usual Istanbul guides.'

His mother's surprise was evident.

'She said the two of you were going to meet anyway, but then she heard that your group needed a guide for Istanbul. They were going to send another guide, but she volunteered — in fact she insisted.'

Once again Etta recalled that Allegra had not known about Kaan's accident until she reached the hotel and found he was not there.

Mrs Talbot's look at Kaan was full of reproach. 'After she had told me everything about the two of you, it was obvious why she had done so. She told me how upset she had been when she heard of your accident. She even told me how happy you were to see her again.'

Kaan was very still.

'What exactly did she tell you about the two of us, what was 'everything'?' he enquired in a very quiet and measured tone.

Mrs Talbot looked almost embarrassed.

'Your relationship — how close you were — how much you meant to each other. She told me how you came to her room one night . . . '

She continued in a rush. 'Really, Kaan, you might have told me about her. She said you didn't because I might not approve of you getting involved with an employee — another employee — but surely you must have known that once I knew you really cared for Allegra . . . '

She stopped, looking at Kaan's set face. 'Isn't it true?'

'I am afraid, Mother,' he said carefully, 'that Allegra may have exaggerated how close we were.'

'But you did go to her room one night . . . ?'

'And she sent me away! Mother, please! Allegra is very beautiful, of course, and I did find her very attractive, but nothing has happened between us.'

'Oh!' was all his mother could say at first, but then a spark of anger appeared. 'Do you mean you have been playing with her, leading her on?'

'Certainly not! I was under the impression that she cared even less about me than I did about her.'

'Perhaps when she heard about your accident she realised how much you meant to her?' his mother offered.

'Perhaps, but I would like to discuss it another time, and certainly not in public like this.' He stood up. 'Now, Etta and I have a lot to do.'

Mrs Talbot obviously wanted to discuss Allegra more, but in view of Kaan's refusal she could not with dignity refuse to go, and was soon gliding away in her limousine, probably brooding on how she had been misled by the beautiful blonde.

Etta was waiting for Kaan when he returned after he had seen his mother to her car.

'That was interesting — ' she began.

'I thought you were eavesdropping,'

he commented curtly and she had the grace to blush.

'Of course. I was surprised to hear that your mother was involved with your office. Why does your mother have anything to do with selecting a guide?'

'She does some work for the tour firm,' he said briefly.

Mrs Talbot certainly hadn't looked as if she needed a part-time job. Perhaps she worked to avoid boredom, or, more probably, to keep an eye on her son.

What Etta was longing to ask — and what was clearly out of the question — was how Kaan really felt about Allegra now.

Was he flattered by her obvious wish to be seen as important to him? He had spoken to his mother as though Allegra no longer meant anything to him, but perhaps he had been unwilling to reveal his true feelings to Mrs Talbot.

And Kaan was meeting Allegra that evening.

8

Etta enjoyed a quiet afternoon alone in her room. She did not feel like dining alone in the hotel, however. She'd had rather a lot of buffet meals in the last few days and anyway, she was curious to see for herself how her mother and George Trent were getting on.

A quick phone call established that her mother would be delighted to see her and that the chauffeur would arrive to collect her at seven o'clock. She had plenty time to shower before coming downstairs early to wait for the car.

Dinner at the hotel was not included for the tourists who had stayed on, but David Trowbridge was having a drink at the bar and rose quickly when he saw her.

'Etta! I hoped I might see you if I waited here.'

Her heart sank. What was the trouble now?

'Can I help you?' she said a little curtly, and he smiled.

'Indeed you can.' He laughed at her expression and put a friendly hand on her arm. 'Relax! All I want you to do is keep me company at dinner. Now Mrs Dankworth is not here to watch our every move, I thought we could enjoy a meal together here.'

'I'm afraid I've already arranged to go out for dinner,' she answered politely.

'That's a pity! But do you have time for a drink with me?'

She looked round. David Trowbridge was much older than she was, and she wasn't at all sure that he was entirely trustworthy. Something about his practised charm reminded her too much of Miles Standing. But there was no sign of Kaan, who had probably gone out already to spend the evening with Allegra.

What harm could there be in having

a drink with David Trowbridge? He obviously wanted her company and that was good for her self-esteem. She had about half-an-hour to wait anyway, and she might find out a little more about him.

Etta smiled. 'I'd love to,' she said.

He proved to be a good companion, full of amusing stories not only about the tourists who had gone, but also about his experiences of other countries. He had obviously travelled widely. Yet all the time she somehow had the impression that she was listening to a well-rehearsed act and she found it difficult to relax completely.

'I've talked about myself a lot,' he commented finally. 'Now tell me something about you. After your experiences during the past couple of weeks, will you be doing tours in the future?'

'Well, so far I've been working in a travel agent's office and I think it has been pretty clear to everyone that this was my first time on a tour,' she explained. 'But I have actually enjoyed this tour and I may ask to do more in the future. It's a good way to get to know a country.'

He nodded. 'And, as I have said before, a tour guide's job can be very rewarding in other ways. After all, you're going from place to place with a set timetable.'

She frowned. 'What do you mean?'

'People don't always want to trust things — letter or parcels, for example — to the post, so they could give them to you to deliver in person.'

'I'm not sure that would be allowed . . .' she began uneasily.

'Who would know? You wouldn't have to tell the travel company.' He leaned forward confidentially. 'I know a few people in Turkey and elsewhere who would be very grateful for such help — and they would pay accordingly.'

'I don't know . . .'

'Where would be the harm? You

don't have to decide now, after all, but I can give you an address where you can contact me any time. It might be profitable for both of us.'

He was very close to her now and she looked round a little desperately for a means of escape. To her great relief she saw her mother's chauffeur, who had just come in the door and was looking round for her.

She waved at him. 'I'm over here!'

David Trowbridge sat back, frowning in evident frustration, then stood up as she rose hastily. She turned to him and held out her hand. 'Thank you. I have enjoyed our talk.'

He took her hand and held on to it long enough to murmur, 'Do think about what I suggested. As I said, no-one would suffer, and you could make some useful money.'

She smiled nervously, nodded, almost dragged her hand from his grasp, and hurried towards the driver.

★   ★   ★

It was a short ride to her stepfather's yacht, where she found her mother and George Trent sitting on deck enjoying the cool evening breeze.

Etta saw her mother look at her and frown slightly at the denim skirt and plain white blouse she was wearing.

'I'm sorry I hadn't anything more suitable to wear,' she apologised. 'My evening clothes were in a suitcase which should have reappeared at our hotel, but hasn't yet.'

'It doesn't matter. There's only the three of us and we're glad to see you whatever you're wearing,' George said comfortably. 'Now, sit down and let me get you a drink.'

It was a very pleasant evening. There was a warmth and intimacy between her mother and George which she had not seen before, and she noticed how often one of them would take the opportunity to touch the other's hand or arm, as if taking pleasure in the simple momentary contact.

Dinner was a long, delicious meal,

served by attentive but unobtrusive staff.

In the past, Etta had always had very little to say when she'd found herself in the couple's company. But to her own pleasant surprise she now found herself describing some of the sights that had impressed her most on the tour, and amusing them with stories about some of the holidaymakers' antics.

'It sounds as though it has been hard work but you've enjoyed yourself,' George commented. 'Would you do it again?'

She thought for a moment and then nodded. 'Yes. I want to go on working in travel. I've seen how important it was to some of the clients, and I definitely need more hands-on experience. Then I can decide whether I want to choose administration or become a travel rep full time.'

'But you must be extremely careful where you go. I wouldn't want you to be sent off to anywhere too primitive . . . ' her mother began solicitously, before she caught her husband's eye and stopped abruptly.

'You mother tells me that you want to come with us when the remaining tourists have left,' George remarked. 'Don't you want to stay in Istanbul for a little longer?'

'I've had enough of hotels for a bit and I feel like a little self-indulgence before I go back home, so yes, I would like to come with you, if you'll have me,' she said, and saw the genuine pleasure on his face.

'We hoped you would decide that,' said George. 'In fact, we have a cabin ready and waiting for you.'

'Then when I've said goodbye to our few remaining clients at the airport I'll take a taxi here.'

'You'll need more clothes, however,' her mother pointed out.

'I know. I thought I might look for a few things tomorrow.'

'We could look for things together,' her mother announced a little uncertainly.

'Why not?' Etta smiled.

Her mother positively beamed. 'How splendid! I haven't been shopping for days.'

George gave a mock groan. 'You have just made your mother very happy,' he informed Etta.

In a rare display of emotion, Etta's mother held her and kissed her goodbye when it was time for her to leave. 'I'll see you tomorrow, then. We'll have a wonderful time.'

As George escorted her to where the car was waiting to take her back to the hotel, Etta tenatively asked, 'You and my mother . . . Is everything all right now?'

'Better than ever. We understand each other now, and we are going to be very happy indeed.' He kissed her forehead and added, 'I'm looking forward to having you with us, Etta.'

★   ★   ★

Back at the hotel, Etta looked round the empty Reception area. 'Is Kaan

Talbot back?' she could not resist enquiring.

The girl half-dozing at the desk shook her head. 'No sign of him yet.' She yawned.

A little of Etta's good mood evaporated.

There was no sign of Kaan at breakfast the next morning. It was possible that he had come back to the hotel, eaten early and gone back to his family's home.

Or perhaps he had not returned because he had spent the night with Allegra.

As she entered the dining room Etta was just in time to see David Trowbridge bent over the table where Burke and Hunt were seated, apparently in deep conversation with them. Burke saw her first, said something quickly, and Trowbridge straightened and walked away from the two men, greeting Etta with a smile.

'I was just saying good morning,' he murmured, as if aware his behaviour needed an explanation. 'After all, with just a few of us left I can't very well ignore them.'

He paused. 'I hope to see you later. Perhaps we can have another drink and continue our interrupted conversation from last night?'

Etta was quite certain that she did not want to spend any more time with him. 'I'm not sure I'll be free,' she told him. 'We have to tie up some paperwork.'

He did not appear too disappointed. 'A pity. After all, it's our last night in Istanbul. We leave tomorrow afternoon.'

'Well at least I'll see you then to say goodbye,' she said with finality, and walked away from him towards the breakfast bar.

Trowbridge left the dining room, and a minute later Burke and Hunt followed.

To her surprise, when she went to take the lift to her room after breakfast, Etta found Kaan also waiting. He looked tired, and there were shadows under his eyes.

'Hello. Did you have a good evening?' she enquired as casually as she could.

'Very pleasant, thank you,' he said formally. 'And you? I understand you were enjoying Mr Trowbridge's conversation.'

'He is a very good companion.'

She knew Kaan was looking at her, but refused to amplify this statement. If he thought she had spent the whole evening with David Trowbridge, then let him!

'I would have thought he was a little old for you,' was Kaan's next remark.

'He's mature, experienced, and amusing.'

They went up in the lift together without saying another word.

Etta had hoped to snatch an hour at the Topkapi Palace by herself, to take another look at its treasures and possibly look into the museum near it, but after breakfast the receptionist informed her that there had been a telephone call from her mother, who would be at the hotel at ten o'clock.

A little later Mrs Trent swished into the hotel wearing an elegant sleeveless white dress set off by a large red handbag embossed with a famous designer's name and greeted Etta with a kiss on both cheeks.

'George is resigned to us spending most of the day shopping,' she announced. 'Do you have the stamina?'

'Of course!' Then her face fell. 'Oh, but I need so much! I really haven't any suitable clothes for the yacht, just a few basic, practical bits.'

Her mother laughed. 'My dear! Why do you think I arranged to come here so early? I've discovered that Istanbul has some very good shops. We can go round them now — and I'm paying! You can call it an early birthday or Christmas present if you like, but please don't start being proud and independent.'

'Mother, I wouldn't dream of it!' Etta said warmly. 'You have a much better dress sense than I have anyway, and I know how much you enjoy shopping for clothes. So let's go and make you and the shopkeepers very happy while I try to survive!'

But Etta was her mother's daughter and like her, she was delighted to spend the next few hours in various very expensive fashion shops. The shops' assistants were also delighted to find that these two customers were as ready to spend as they were to search through their stock.

'You can dump everything you brought with you,' Mrs Trent informed Etta. 'They are working clothes, after all, and you're going to be on holiday now.'

By the end of a long morning Etta felt she had been equipped for every possible occasion, and her mother had also incidentally acquired a few garments for herself.

Over a light lunch, Mrs Trent frowned over their list of purchases. 'We did get you some evening sandals, didn't we?'

'Yes, and I thought we were going to

sail, not socialise.'

'Oh, there are bound to be a few parties when people meet in the yacht clubs.' Another frown. 'We don't seem to have a glamorous short dress, but someone told me there's a good shop about five minutes' walk from here.'

Etta wiggled her toes. 'Can we make that the last shop, then? My feet are getting tired.'

Mrs Trent had a determined gleam in her eye. 'I've heard good things about this shop, and it isn't far and you must have a short dress. You can rest later.

'Incidentally, George and I thought you might like to have dinner with us again on the yacht tonight — unless you have to do something for those people you have been dragging around.'

'Well, thank you both for the invitation, but I'd better stay in the hotel in case there are any last-minute emergencies with the remaining tourists. I don't know how many I'll see because they don't have to eat in the hotel, but that doesn't mean there won't be some need for our help.'

From her frown, her mother was obviously about to make some criticism, but then she hesitated and shrugged. 'Very well, you do your duty. Now, let's go and find this last shop.'

Etta reflected happily that George's advice was obviously having some effect.

The dress shop was small, tucked away discreetly down a side street, with one elegant black dress displayed in the window. There was no price tag.

As they went in, Mrs Trent looked round and smiled happily. This was her kind of shop! Instead of racks of dresses there were just three dressmakers' models beautifully attired, complete with every accessory. A woman whose elegance matched that of the models came forward and offered her help.

Mrs Trent explained that they were looking for a dress, short but suitable for evening wear, for her daughter. The woman looked at Etta steadily for a few seconds, then invited them to sit down in two comfortable armchairs while she found something they might consider suitable among the stock.

Within five minutes two assistants were bringing out a series of dresses for Mrs Trent and Etta to inspect. They were the correct size, and all very desirable.

After some enjoyable inspections and hesitations, Mrs Trent and the saleswoman narrowed the selection down to four, remembering to ask Etta for her opinion but not always taking any notice of it.

Etta tried all four on in turn, marvelling at how they flattered her. She twirled in front of the mirror. If Kaan saw her in one of these, she found herself thinking, he might even forget Allegra for a few seconds.

Mrs Trent, however, was still not completely satisified. 'I like this style,' she said, indicating one of the dresses with a perfectly manicured finger, 'but I would prefer it in *that* colour.' The finger pointed at a blue-green creation.

The woman shook her head regretfully. 'I am afraid we do not have that particular dress in the blue-green colour, Madam.'

A small frown appeared between Mrs Trent's eyes, but Etta said hastily, 'It doesn't matter. I'll take both anyway, since they're all beautiful.'

Mrs Trent appeared reluctant to settle for anything less than perfection, but just at that moment, before Etta could make her final choice, the door opened and a woman in a flowing blue dress entered.

The assistants almost stood to attention when they saw her and Etta recognised the newcomer instantly. It was Kaan's mother, Mrs Talbot. She looked at Etta, then looked again and frowned, obviously aware she had seen her before, but unable to remember exactly where.

Etta moved towards her, smiling. 'Mrs Talbot! I met you the other evening. I was the one who had to tell you that Kaan had had an accident. I'm so glad it wasn't serious.'

Mrs Talbot's face cleared and she smiled warmly. 'Why, yes, of course! You are Etta. Kaan told me many good things about you last night.'

And Etta knew from his mother's attitude that he had been complimentary. But if he had been speaking to his mother last night, what had happened to Allegra?

Mrs Trent, not used to being ignored, coughed discreetly at this moment, and Etta turned to include her in the conversation.

'May I introduce my mother, Mrs Trent? Mother, this is Mrs Talbot, Kaan's mother.'

The two women smiled, but their eyes were busy making a rapid inventory of each other's appearance from carefully-styled hair to designer shoes. Apparently both were satisfied with what they saw, for their smiles grew wider and warmer.

'I saw you the other evening,' Mrs Trent said, 'but Etta didn't have a chance to introduce us because you had to hurry off to the hospital to see how your son was after his accident. I was so glad to hear that he has fully recovered.'

Mrs Talbot sighed. 'I am sorry about that, but at least we have met properly now and I can thank your daughter for the way she coped with that emergency.'

'Are you looking for something to wear?' Mrs Trent asked. 'I have been most impressed by the stock here.'

Etta was conscious of the three shop assistants visibly brightening at her words.

'I'm delighted to hear that,' said Mrs Talbot. 'In fact I often acquire my dresses here because I happen to own the shop. I hope you have found something you like.'

Mrs Talbot owned this shop as well as being interested in the tour firm! Something else to think about.

'Yes, thank you,' said Etta, but Mrs Trent was sighing, shaking her head.

'I thought we had found the ideal

dress for my daughter, but unfortunately you haven't got her size in the colour we want.'

Mrs Talbot looked sharply at the head assistant, who hurriedly explained the unfortunate lack of the right combination.

Kaan's mother waved her hand airily. 'There is no problem. We will have that style made up in that colour for your daughter.'

Etta saw the head assistant open her mouth as if to protest but then hastily close it again.

Mrs Trent was still frowning. 'But won't that take some time? We are expecting to sail in a few days.'

'It will be ready the day after tomorrow,' promised Mrs Talbot without hesitation. 'I shall contact the workshop myself.'

Etta murmured her thanks to Mrs Talbot, a little embarrassed, especially when Mrs Trent produced her credit card, only to have it waved aside.

'The dress will be a gift,' she told

Etta and her mother. 'To show my thanks for the help your daughter has given my son. Now, if you will give the assistant details of your cruise liner . . . '

'Not a liner — my husband's yacht,' Mrs Trent said crisply, and Mrs Talbot gave her another long, thoughtful look.

'Oh, but I couldn't take the dress as a gift!' Etta protested, but both Mrs Talbot and Mrs Trent ignored her, so it was obviously pointless to protest further.

The necessary details were exchanged, and Etta and her mother left the shop, smiling and thanking Mrs Talbot, their mission accomplished.

'Mother, I should have paid for the dress,' Etta said, still feeling uneasy. 'It was very expensive.'

'Nonsense! Never refuse a freebie, even if you can afford to pay,' her mother said firmly. 'Besides, as Mrs Talbot said, it was a gift to thank you for helping this young man, Kaan, so you must let her show her gratitude.

'Anyway, his mother can obviously afford it,' she went on. 'Her dress was silk, and that handbag was very expensive. And did you notice her watch? A Rolex!' She grew thoughtful. 'I only saw this Kaan briefly,' she commented, 'but I did tell you to find out more about him. Is he an acceptable young man?'

'I'm not sure what you mean by that. He is intelligent and very competent. All the clients think he's marvellous.'

'Well-educated?'

'I suppose he must be — and his table manners are very good, just in case you are wondering!'

Her mother was only half-listening. 'I think I'd like to meet this young man again,' she said reflectively.

'Well you can't. We're taking the last few clients to the airport tomorrow and then I shall probably never see him again.'

'But you must think of something,' her mother ordered. 'Get his email address at least. You should definitely keep in contact after what you have been through together.'

If only she could! But what use would that be? 'Mother, he already has a very beautiful girlfriend.'

'So? You'll just have to make him change his mind. I never found that difficult to do.'

Etta was silent on the journey back to the hotel, thinking about Kaan's unexpectedly opulent mother.

Mrs Trent gave her a brief parting kiss and left her at the hotel entrance before returning to the yacht in a taxi almost filled with her purchases.

Etta went slowly into the hotel and the first person she saw was Kaan, slumped in a chair reading a newspaper. He raised a weary hand in greeting and she sat down beside him, refusing his polite offer of a coffee.

'I've drunk gallons of hotel coffee since I came to Turkey.'

'Travel reps can always go without food if necessary, but they need caffeine,' Kaan declared.

'Kaan, I want you to explain some things.'

'Can't they wait? I really must do that laundry,' said Kaan, half-rising, but Etta's hand gripped his arm firmly.

'The washing can wait a few minutes, Kaan. I really want a word with you. Please sit down.'

He did as he was told looking at her cautiously. 'What is it?'

'I met your mother again today.' He stared at her. 'In fact, my mother and I met her in a very up-market dress shop and it turned out that she is the owner. And from what you have said she also seems to have some connection with the travel firm.'

Kaan fidgeted, seemed about to rise, and then sank back.

'Oh, well, I suppose I should tell you the full truth about my family now.' He sighed and began to explain. 'My mother is a very capable and intelligent woman. When she came back to Istanbul after my father died she didn't need to work, but after a while she was bored stiff and restless and started looking for something to occupy her.

'Well, friends and in-laws from England were always coming to visit her and asking her advice on the best way to see Turkey, so she started organising tours of Istanbul. Gradually the tours grew larger, until now they cover all Turkey. Mother still owns the tour company, but she loves clothes, so eventually she also set up her own dress shop . . . '

He gave a limp smile and added, 'And I might as well tell you that there is also a language school teaching English to Turks and Turkish to the English. When it was time for me to choose a career I decided on tourism and I am in charge of a lot of that part of the family business now.'

'So when you are not touring with the groups you help run it? So you can't go on many tours?' Etta surmised.

'Nowadays I only go on tours occasionally, just to see if everything is working all right, and whether there is anything we could do to improve the experience. When I do that I try to appear like an ordinary tour guide, as I did to you.'

He stood up and said rather sharply, 'Is that all? I really do have a couple of shirts to wash, you know.'

Etta shook her head. 'You know I don't like unfinished stories. For example, there's Allegra, who, having turned you down flat, was suddenly only too eager to help you and meet you again. When you saw her last night, did you find out why she had changed her mind about you?'

Kaan sighed and sat down again.

'Etta, after what I've just told you, you must be able to guess the answer to that as easily as I did. You yourself know what it's like when people find out you have a wealthy parent.

'When Allegra started working regularly for Top Turkish Tours in Istanbul after her encounter with me, she soon found out that the tour guide she had rejected was actually the heir to a flourishing company and would probably end up as the owner of three well-established businesses.

'Allegra likes money and she must have been furious with herself for turning me down. So when she heard of my accident it must have seemed a chance sent from heaven to get back with me — and if she could get my mother on her side as well, so much the better!'

Etta tried to control herself but it was no use. She found herself laughing. Kaan was obviously not amused and gazed at her stonily.

'I can't help it,' she giggled. 'It's this mental picture of the rich, handsome prince, pretending to be a commoner, constantly pursued by beautiful women who want his money when they find out who he really is.'

His glare vanished as his mouth began to twitch. 'Just like a fairy story — and I'm pleased that you think I'm handsome! And incidentally,' he added as his grin broadened, 'aren't you the

258

princess in disguise?'

She ignored his comment. 'So what are you going to do about Allegra?'

He looked at her from under lowered eyelashes. 'She has obviously changed her opinion of me . . . perhaps I might take advantage of that.'

It was not what Etta wanted to hear. How could she rival Allegra? Then she felt his warm touch as he took her hand in his.

'I was only teasing, Etta! Last night, as she made sure you knew, I took her out to dinner.'

'Oh,' Etta said flatly.

'Listen! I thanked her for her help but told her that in future our relationship, if any, would be strictly a working one.'

Etta gazed at him in genuine astonishment. 'But she's so beautiful! How could you resist her?'

'That is what she seemed to think, too,' he laughed. 'It took some time but I managed to finally convince her that I was no longer interested in her.'

'How?'

He avoided her gaze. 'I told her I'd met someone else.'

It was like a physical blow. 'Why did you say that?'

'Because I have.'

It was at that moment, when his simple statement destroyed any hopes she might have had that she could interest him, that Etta realised how much she had come to care for him.

Before she could gather her thoughts he stood up, clearly determined to leave before she could ask him more, and in doing so he accidentally brushed his newspaper off the table. He picked the paper up and then stared at the headlines, frowning slightly.

'Have you seen this? Yet another robbery. Safe deposit boxes broken into in a bank. It means the thieves got away with any gold and jewellery from the boxes, but didn't take any paper money which might be traceable.

'It's surprising how many similar robberies there have been recently in the area we cover, but fortunately we do warn people against bringing valuables with them.'

Thinking Kaan was merely trying to change the subject, Etta managed from between tight lips to mutter, 'Well if Mr Hunt hears about it he'll be clutching his bag to him even more tightly,' before watching his tall figure walk away from her.

9

Etta dressed carefully for the last dinner at the hotel. She had told her mother it was her duty to stay, and so it was, she told herself. But it was probable that Kaan would be there that evening, and it would be her last chance to spend some time with him. The next day, after a quick breakfast, they would escort the remaining clients to the airport and then she and Kaan would separate.

She would take a taxi to her stepfather's yacht, and Kaan would return to the tour offices, presumably — unless he went to meet his unknown girlfriend. What was she like, this mystery woman who could make him reject Allegra, and why had he never mentioned her before?

When she went downstairs for her meal, after checking her appearance very carefully and deciding at last that she was satisfied, her heart sank, because there was nobody there that she recognised. She took her seat at a small table, resigned to a lonely evening, then suddenly heard a voice behind her.

'Miss Sanderson! Etta! You can't sit there by yourself. Come and join us.'

It was the Elliotts, a middle-aged couple who had toured Turkey with undisguised enthusiasm, photographing absolutely everything. She accepted their offer gratefully.

'Have you enjoyed exploring Istanbul?' she asked.

'It's been marvellous. We took so many pictures that we had to buy another disk for our camera. Of course, we didn't manage to see everything. In fact, I think we might come back some time and do the tour again.'

'With the same company?'

'Why, yes indeed! We've been very well looked after.'

Mrs Elliott looked past Etta, smiled, and waved a hand in greeting. 'Hello!

We wondered where you'd go for the night.'

Another middle-aged couple had appeared and joined them.

'Well, it's an early start tomorrow, so we didn't want to go too far from the hotel, and we thought it might be a good chance to have a last drink to mark the end of the holiday with some of the people we've got to know.'

Then another couple came into the restaurant, and before long all the remaining clients were assembled — with the exceptions of Burke and Hunt and David Trowbridge, and nobody seemed to miss them. On a smaller scale, it was a repetition of the earlier farewell evening.

Finally, just as Etta was giving up hope, Kaan appeared and received a warm welcome from the group.

'We thought you were avoiding us, that you'd had enough of us,' someone said, but Kaan laughed and shook his head.

'Avoid such charming people? Of

course not! I just went home to see my mother first.'

Etta found that she was smiling. So his mother had come before the girlfriend — unless, of course, she had been at his mother's house ... Her smile vanished abruptly.

Dinner was a long, noisy meal. One man insisted on trying to make a farewell speech to everybody until his wife pulled him back down into his seat.

Etta was sitting next to a middle-aged Australian woman and her husband; a quiet couple she'd had little to do with during the tour, mostly because they had made no demands and had nothing to complain about.

'Are you going back to Australia soon?' she asked politely, but the woman shook her head.

'Not for six weeks. We're going to visit relatives in England, then we're going to Paris and afterwards to Prague and Vienna. Then we're cruising down the Nile. In fact, we'll be away from home for three months altogether.'

Her eyes were shining. 'Arthur and I have always wanted to travel, but we were too busy working and bringing up the children. But we agreed that when he retired we would go everywhere we'd dreamed of going, so five years ago we began to make our plans and save up. Two weeks after Arthur stopped work we took a plane to America.'

'And has the world lived up to your expectations?'

'We've loved every moment! All the effort and money it took to achieve this holiday has been worthwhile.' She patted Etta's hand. 'And a lot of that has been due to people like you and Kaan, looking after us and telling us so many interesting things about everything. Thank you.'

Etta realised guiltily that she had often overlooked the fact that although she saw this temporary job as a way of proving herself, its real purpose was to help other people enjoy their holiday experience to the full — and she realised that that was a really worth-while aim.

Afterwards the group moved to the bar, and it looked as if some would be doing their early-morning packing with sore heads. Kaan and Etta managed to refuse most of the drinks offered to them.

'Well, to all intents and purposes this is the end of the tour,' Kaan said with a trace of regret when they found themselves alone for a few minutes. 'They can swallow a few aspirins and nurse their headaches on the flight home — and you won't be on the plane feeling responsible for them any more.'

He paused, and then said a little stiffly, 'I understand you've decided against staying on in Istanbul and that you'll be going to join your mother and her husband on their yacht instead . . . '

'I did mean to tell you! How do you know that?'

'Oh, Mother told me all about your meeting in her shop. If I'd known that evening when you arrived that you had such rich relations I might have treated you with more respect,' Kaan said with undisguised sarcasm.

'Well, you didn't tell me about your own mother's flourishing businesses!' She looked down, avoiding his eyes and suddenly feeling coy. 'Anyway, I thought you'd be too busy to bother with me if I stayed in Istanbul.'

'Why would you think that?'

'Well, you might prefer the company of your mystery girlfriend.' She looked up at him, entreaty in her eyes. 'Come on, Kaan. We're not going to see each other again after tomorrow morning, so why not tell me about her? Who is this girlfriend you prefer to Allegra? She must be very special. Why haven't you mentioned her before?'

He was silent for a moment before he looked at her with mock indignation.

'Aren't you forgetting your place, Miss Sanderson? You're not supposed to ask your boss about his love life.'

As her eyes flashed he leaned forward, suddenly very serious, and took her hand. 'But at the airport tomorrow, Etta, when we have said goodbye to everyone, you will no longer be an employee and I will tell you the name of the girl I love then.'

She looked at him uncertainly, suddenly not sure whether she wanted to know. 'You really don't have to. I was just being overly inquisitive.'

He smiled. 'I think I want to, though I'm not sure what your reaction will be.' He sat back and looked round at the cheerful crowd. 'Now, we have to be sober and responsible tomorrow morning, so shall we slip away quietly?'

One or two people waved goodbye as they left.

'You've been really good reps,' the frustrated speech-maker called out, standing up rather unsteadily. 'In fact we all think you make a good couple, actually!' He laughed raucously as his wife could be heard telling him to sit down and be quiet.

Etta walked out into the reception area with her cheeks burning at the remark — just in time to see Burke and Hunt coming in the front doors.

'Just look!' she said, eager to distract Kaan. 'That man is still carrying his shoulder bag!'

'I wonder if he carries it around all the time in England?' Kaan said flippantly.

At that moment, close behind the other two men, David Trowbridge also came into the hotel. As Etta and Kaan watched, the three newcomers got into the same lift.

'Trowbridge always seems to laugh at those two, says he doesn't want to be in their company, but he's very often near to them,' Kaan said thoughtfully as they waited for the next lift.

'I have told you about the times I've seen all three of them together,' Etta reminded him, 'and they always seemed to have plenty to talk about.'

'Well, we won't have to bother about any of them after tomorrow morning.'

When the lift reached their floor they said goodnight and Kaan walked away towards his room. Etta stood still, looking after him, trying to memorise the way he looked and moved.

He looked over his shoulder, saw her standing there and half-turned, as if he were about to come back and speak to her. Then he shrugged, gave a half-wave, and went on walking away.

★   ★   ★

Etta lay awake for a long time, brooding over the tour.

When it had begun it seemed to stretch ahead for a long, long time, but it had in fact passed very quickly. She had learned invaluable lessons on how to handle people and awkward situations, as well as experiencing everything from delight at ancient masterpieces to horror as Kaan had lain motionless and bloody on the coach floor.

But she knew that it was Kaan she would remember for ever, not only for his golden eyes and the natural grace of his tall body, but for their conflicts and reconciliations, their moments of comradeship and empathy.

She told herself not to be stupid. He was the only young, attractive man she had worked closely with and what she felt was infatuation and gratitude, which would quickly fade once she left Turkey.

But it felt like love.

She sat up and thumped her pillow into a more comfortable position. Suppose it was love — what then? He cared for someone else, so that was the end of any hopes she might have cherished, so she would just have to get over it.

Anyway, she would have plenty to distract her and cheer her up. Tomorrow she would board her stepfather's yacht for a luxurious cruise round the Mediterranean, and when she went back to work she would be able to show that she was no longer just the poor little rich girl playing at work but someone who could be a useful member of the team.

Tomorrow would mark the end of one stage in her life and the beginning of the next.

★ ★ ★

The alarm clock woke her early enough to shower and pack. She simply crammed her clothes into her suitcase, resolving that she would dump the lot once the fashionable clothes she and her mother had bought were delivered, then took it down in the lift to Reception, where the case would be collected by their coach driver.

Kaan was already finishing his breakfast and gave her a distracted smile and a brief greeting as he went out.

The remaining clients were thin on the ground and those who did come in seemed to want just coffee more than anything else. After breakfast, she checked with Reception that all bills had been paid and there were no complaints or problems, and went back to her own room to collect her blazer and bag.

She looked in the mirror carefully to see if the tour had made any physical changes to her, wondering how Kaan would remember her. Well, she had acquired a golden tan and had definitely lost a few pounds in weight. Any other changes, to the ways she thought and acted, were not visible but would prove much more important.

She sighed, picked up her bag and looked round the small, anonymous hotel room. It was adequate, but the yacht would definitely be better.

Downstairs the clients were beginning to assemble and Kaan was checking his lists and repeating the details of the flight times and the procedure at the airport.

He turned to Hunt, who was still clutching his shoulder bag.

'I'm afraid you'll have to part with your bag for a few seconds at check-in, Mr Hunt. Remember, your hand luggage goes through the scanner, so don't try to smuggle out any of our antiques,' he joked.

Hunt scowled at him but did not reply.

Lastly, Kaan looked at Etta. 'Give me that blazer,' he said.

She handed over the ugly garment and he held it up, laughed, and dropped it in a nearby waste paper basket. 'I don't think you need that any longer, Etta. We can all recognise you now.'

For the last time they all climbed into the coach and Etta took her familiar seat beside Kaan. The driver twisted the steering-wheel and slowly they left the hotel and were soon on the main thoroughfare that would take them out of Istanbul to the airport.

The adventure was finally ending.

There was the usual ritual of checking that everybody had their passport and ticket handy, and the short wait while Kaan located their check-in desk.

Standing by the desk, helping with

any problems such as overweight luggage crammed with souvenirs, would be their last service for this little group whom they had come to know well in such a short time.

Most of the tourists were seasoned travellers so there were no serious hitches and almost all had surrendered their bags, said goodbye to Kaan and Etta and made for the departure lounge, with everything going very smoothly.

Burke and Hunt, and then David Trowbridge, were the last three in the queue. It was Hunt's turn to check in. He swung his suitcase on the conveyor belt and it easily passed the weight test. Obviously he had not bothered to buy many souvenirs. Then, obediently but with obvious reluctance, he held up his shoulder bag so that the clerk could see that it was suitable as carry-on hand luggage.

At this moment, as the clerk was nodding approval, Etta, who had been staring at the bag, stepped forward. She had wondered whether to say anything but decided she had to intervene. 'Mr Hunt, that's not your bag!' she cried out.

He clutched the bag to him, then swung round and glared at her while Kaan looked at her in surprise and the clerk hesitated.

'Don't be stupid. You've seen me carrying this all round Turkey. Everybody knows this is my bag.'

Burke nodded his agreement and tried to create a diversion by shouldering Etta aside and lifting his own case on to the conveyor belt, but she stood her ground.

'That case isn't the one you've had for the rest of the trip, Mr Hunt. The one you've been carrying around had blue piping in the seams, but this one has black.'

Hunt shook his head violently. 'You don't know what you're talking about!'

But now Kaan, suddenly alert, spoke up firmly and confidently. 'Miss Sanderson is right about the colour of the piping. That bag is not the one you've been clutching during your entire holiday.'

'Nonsense! Stop holding everyone up and let's get on with the check-in,' Burke almost snarled.

The clerk looked from Kaan to Hunt, obviously wondering what to do next.

'It's easy enough to make sure. Open the bag and see what's inside,' Etta told Hunt, refusing to be worried by his aggressive stance now that Kaan had openly confirmed what she had noticed.

He hugged the bag to him, his face red with fury. A nearby security guard, scenting trouble, had drifted closer and when Hunt saw this it seemed to upset him even more.

'I'm not showing everybody what I've got in my bag! It's my bag, I tell you!'

Now the clerk also sensed trouble and was unobtrusively beckoning the security guard nearer.

'It would be better if you opened the bag, sir,' she suggested to Hunt. 'You don't want to get on the plane and then find you've got the wrong one.'

Hunt snarled at her and the guard obviously decided it was time to intervene. 'Please, open the bag, sir,' he instructed.

Hunt held his bag even more tightly and it was becoming clear to everyone that the situation had gone beyond an irritated traveller annoyed with what he saw as unnecessary checks. There was something seriously wrong.

Suddenly Hunt turned, looking round as if for help, and surprisingly he appealed not to Burke or Kaan but to David Trowbridge, standing behind them, the last in the queue.

'What do I do?' Hunt asked him urgently.

David Trowbridge lifted an eyebrow and frowned slightly. 'Why ask me? It's nothing to do with me.'

'Don't give me that! You have to help me!'

Trowbridge's face was suddenly a mask of fury. 'I don't know what you're talking about!'

279

At that moment, while Hunt confronted Trowbridge and they were distracted, the security guard stretched out his hand and neatly twitched the shoulder bag from Hunt's hands.

Hunt cursed and tried to grab the bag back, but the guard held it out of his reach.

'Come with me to the office,' he ordered. 'We can sort this matter out in private.'

Hunt did not move to follow the guard but looked round desperately and then suddenly leaped at the man, sending him to the ground.

He snatched the shoulder bag back and broke away, running for the nearby exit, closely followed by Burke. But before he could reach the doors, a shout from the fallen guard sent two other security men running to intercept the pair, and while everyone else in the check-in area watched in fascinated horror, tackles worthy of any rugby game brought them both down before they could reach the doors.

They did not give in even then, and there were scuffles as they still fought wildly to escape, but as more guards appeared they were hopelessly outnumbered and finally lay on the floor, cursing steadily, while the guards first handcuffed them and then stood over them with pistols drawn.

As the guards seized the two men, the attention of everyone in the departure hall was fixed on the scene, but suddenly Etta's right wrist was gripped and she found she was being pulled towards the exit and through the doors by David Trowbridge.

'Wait! What are you doing?' she cried out in alarm.

'It's safer out here,' he told her, still gripping her wrist.

She looked at him. He was sweating profusely and his eyes were darting from side to side as if looking for an escape route. Was he trying to protect her or had the violence scared him? Whatever the reason, she was still responsible for him until he reached the departures lounge.

'It's all over now. We can go back,' she said in what she hoped was a calm and soothing voice. 'But you still have to check in, Mr Trowbridge.'

But now his grip on her wrist was painful and he was dragging her among a stand of parked cars, bending his head as if to avoid being seen.

'Mr Trowbridge! Let me go!'

She dug in her heels so that he was forced to stop, and when he turned to her his teeth were bared in an expression of vicious savagery. 'I'm keeping you with me,' he hissed. 'The guards won't attack me if I'm using you as a shield.'

At that moment she heard Kaan's voice calling her name and she opened her mouth to call back but Trowbridge held up his free hand menacingly.

'Make a noise and I'll hit you — hard!' he threatened.

As his hand touched her face she turned her head and bit down on his fingers until her teeth felt resistance and he screamed in pain.

When his grip slackened momentarily, she tore herself free and started to run away, dodging between the cars with Trowbridge in hot pursuit.

She heard Kaan calling again, a note of panic in his voice.

'I'm here, Kaan, I'm here!' she shrieked.

Trowbridge was almost on her when there was the thud of heavy boots on the ground and two guards appeared in front of them. Trowbridge turned, but three more were behind them and he stood still, his shoulders drooping sullenly, until the guards seized him and led him away.

Etta suddenly found herself in Kaan's arms and, as she sobbed with relief, his hand caressed her shoulders and he was murmuring softly to her, his face buried in her hair.

She could not make out the words but his soothing tone comforted her and she stayed passive and content in his embrace until a guard came up and spoke to him.

Kaan held her hand and led her back inside the airport building to a small room. Here, after she had assured Kaan that she was all right except for a bruised wrist, an official brought her a cup of hot, sweet tea.

'It's good for shock,' Kaan assured her.

'It was a shock. I wondered what on earth he was doing?'

'He was desperate and taking you as hostage seemed the only way out, I suppose. Burke and Hunt were claiming that he was their boss and his trying to run away like that seems to confirm their claim.'

He looked at his watch and grinned. 'Well, at least in ten minutes' time the rest of our clients will be boarding their plane, blissfully unaware of the drama they missed, because they'd all gone into the departure lounge before you spotted the difference in Hunt's bag.'

Her own shoulder bag had been retrieved and restored to her, and after a while a policeman came in and spoke to Kaan, who nodded quietly.

'The police want to talk to me because they want all the information I can give,' he told Etta. 'It may take some time.'

'What about me?'

'Wait here and I'll come back for you as soon as I can.'

He left, and an hour passed very slowly. The official fidgeted and offered her more tea, which she declined.

'It looks as if your friend is going to be gone for longer than he expected,' the official commented. 'Do you have somewhere to go? You're a travel rep, so I suppose you are staying at a hotel, but after your experience I would prefer you to go somewhere where there is someone to look after you.'

There was only one person in Istanbul who would give her shelter and care.

'My mother is in Istanbul, at least her husband's yacht is,' she replied distractedly. 'She'll look after me.'

'Excellent. Now if you'll just tell me

how to contact her . . . '

But this was where her difficulties really began. Etta knew the name of the yacht — after all, it was named after her mother — but she could not remember how to describe exactly where it was moored. She had her mother's mobile phone number, but there was no answer when she called and the official was beginning to frown.

Then, suddenly, the door was thrown open and her mother appeared in person, arms outstretched, and Etta found herself engulfed in a passionate hug.

'Oh, my love! What's been going on? There are policemen everywhere and I was told you'd been attacked. Are you all right? It's like some gangster film.'

A delayed reaction to the scene at the check-in suddenly hit Etta and she burst into tears as she cuddled into the shelter of her mother's arms.

'He hurt me! That man hurt me!'

Her mother's arms tightened until Etta flinched.

'Where are you hurt? Show me!'

Etta tried to pull herself together. 'There's nothing much wrong with me, really, Mother, but you're hurting all my bruises!'

As Mrs Trent's grip slackened Etta saw over her mother's shoulder that Mrs Talbot was also entering the room.

'I can't find my son anywhere,' she was complaining. 'Someone said he's helping the police. They made it sound as though he had been arrested but I said that was impossible.'

Mrs Trent released her hold on Etta, who sank back on the couch again.

'Kaan called his mother and told her that you had been attacked at the airport and asked her to tell me,' Mrs Trent explained at last. 'He knew she had the details of how to contact me after we had been in her shop.'

'Kaan is obviously too involved in what is happening to look after you himself,' Mrs Talbot interrupted, 'so instead of just telephoning your mother I had myself driven to her yacht, where

I gave her the news, and then we both came here in my car as quickly as possible.'

Mrs Trent was inspecting Etta's wrist, frowning deeply.

'That is a very nasty bruise. I'll take you to the yacht to rest and then we'll get a doctor to come and see you.'

'No! I want to stay here and find out what's happening.'

Mrs Trent shook her head impatiently. 'You can't wait here at the airport. Whatever the matter is, it's nothing to do with you anyway and they've probably all gone off to some police station to sort it all out.'

'And I'm afraid I need my room free,' added the official, who was beginning to look a little harassed.

'I'm not leaving until I find out what is happening to Kaan!'

The two mothers looked at Etta, then at each other, and then Mrs Talbot produced a solution.

'You must both come with me,' she announced. 'My house is much nearer anyway and will be much more convenient. Besides, wherever Kaan is and whatever he is doing, eventually he must come home, and then we will all find out everything.'

'My husband is expecting us . . . ' began Mrs Trent.

'You can call him and tell him what is happening,' Mrs Talbot suggested help-fully.

Faced with Etta, Mrs Talbot and the impatient official, Mrs Trent had no choice but to capitulate and phoned her husband to inform him where she was going.

In spite of Etta's protests that she could manage perfectly well by herself, the chauffeur was summoned to sup-port her to the car, and with Mrs Talbot and Mrs Trent both fussing round her, the little group slowly made its way to the exit, with Etta keenly aware of people turning to stare at their progress.

Everything was proceeding normally in the check-in area, with no sign of the recent drama. In the car park where the limousine was waiting Etta was tenderly installed in the generous back seat, and as the vehicle glided off she lay back, cuddled in her mother's arms, and a few tears slowly crept down her cheeks, as reaction to the morning's events finally set in.

10

The car drove through tall gates in a high brick wall and drew up in front of what looked like a simple single-storey building whose whitewashed wall was broken only by two small windows and a large wooden door, which was opened by a maid.

Once inside the door, Etta and Mrs Trent stopped and gasped. They were in an impressive entrance hall, from which a broad staircase led downwards. Looking straight ahead, dominating everything, huge windows looked out over the Bosphorus. Etta and her mother realised as Mrs Talbot led them into an enormous airy sitting room that the house was actually a two-storey edifice built on a slope overlooking the Bosphorus, with the entrance on the upper floor.

Mrs Talbot seated her guests, sent the

maid for refreshments, and then insisted that a doctor should be sent for to inspect Etta's wrist. 'That man may have damaged a tendon or crushed something.'

The doctor arrived within minutes and both mothers insisted on watching as he checked Etta's wrist with cool, gentle hands and finally pronounced that there was no serious damage, but that she would have some very painful bruises.

He offered to leave her something to help her sleep but she shook her head. 'No, I don't want to sleep. I want to stay awake until Kaan comes back. I want to know what he has to tell me.'

She looked at the two mothers with entreaty in her eyes but they would not support her.

'He may not be back till very late, and by then you'll be too tired to take anything in,' Mrs Talbot pointed out.

'I'll be perfectly all right. I'm not a baby.'

'Of course not,' her mother said soothingly. 'Shall we get you a nice cup of tea?' Unseen by Etta, she gave Mrs Talbot a look full of meaning and the other woman nodded.

At this offer Etta suddenly realised that she wanted a fresh, hot cup of tea more than anything in the world. She smiled gratefully, the tea arrived after a short delay, was poured into a delicate china cup, and she drank it with great pleasure. It was only five minutes later, as sleep began to engulf her, that she realised that the tea had contained the sleeping pills.

★　★　★

Etta woke in semi-darkness, yawned and stretched, wondering where she was, then realised she was in a bed and stretched an exploratory arm out of the coverlet. There was a rustle of clothes and she turned her head to see a young woman bending over her, smiling.

She blinked at the unfamiliar face, but before she could ask any questions the girl had moved away. She heard a door open and shut, and then it was reopened and there was the familiar quick click of heels approaching the bed.

Her mother leaned over her, kissed her very gently, and then briskly opened the curtains to admit bright sunlight before turning to inspect her daughter at leisure.

'So you're awake at last, Etta! We were beginning to worry that we'd put too many tablets in your tea.'

Etta propped herself on her elbows and glared. 'You mean you doped me? You knew I wanted to stay awake until Kaan came home! What's the time?'

'Six o'clock.'

Etta jerked upright, was overcome by dizziness, and fell back on her abundant pillows. 'Six o'clock? What's happened? Where's Kaan? Is everything all right?'

Mrs Trent perched on the side of the bed. 'He still hasn't returned, but he did phone . . . '

'What did he tell you?' interrupted Etta. 'Is he all right?'

Her mother sighed heavily. 'As I was saying, Kaan did phone, but his mother said that apparently all he could do was mumble that it was very complicated, and he didn't expect to be back for several hours yet.'

'Was that all? Did he ask about me?'

'That was one of the few things he did manage to ask. Mrs Talbot told him there was nothing to worry about. Now, your bathroom is over there, so if you'd like to freshen up you can join me and Mrs Talbot and then we can go back to the yacht.'

Etta rinsed her face and hands and made her way out into the rest of the house. It was big, and confusing, and Etta was grateful when a young maid appeared and guided her to a balcony overlooking the garden where Mrs Talbot and Mrs Trent, reclining on comfortable chairs, were chatting like old friends.

Mrs Talbot seemed unconcerned by her son's continued absence, sure that he could cope. 'You'll hear as soon as we do, so relax and enjoy the view,' she told Etta, waving a hand at the splendour before them.

The Talbots' house was surrounded by gardens on three sides, and the panoramic views of the Bosphorus dominated everything. Etta remembered what Allegra had said on the cruise up this waterway about the cost of such houses and could not help speculating briefly on exactly how wealthy the Talbots were.

Etta suspected that, apart from maternal anxiety, her mother had been delighted to have an excuse to visit such a gorgeous house and get to know more about it. Even by Mrs Trent's demanding standards, it was superb.

When Mrs Talbot excused herself to go and supervise some domestic activity, this was confirmed when Etta's mother stretched out her slim legs and commented, 'I like this place very much.' She looked sideways at Etta. 'And apparently Kaan is Mrs Talbot's only son.'

Etta looked at her grimly. 'Don't start

dreaming of weddings, Mother, because you'll be disappointed. Kaan already has a girlfriend. Not the one I told you about — another one.'

Her mother looked surprised. 'Are you sure? His mother doesn't seem to know that.'

'Well, presumably he'll tell her sometime — when he finally gets back.'

But Kaan still did not appear and Mrs Trent reluctantly began to think about getting back to the yacht and her husband.

'This is a lovely house, and I would like to stay here longer,' she said a little wistfully, 'but we do have some friends from another yacht coming for drinks later tonight. In fact, Etta, I think you should come back to the yacht with me now and Kaan can call you to tell you his story.'

'I want to stay here until Kaan gets back,' Etta said plaintively. She could not explain to her mother how heart-broken she would be if her last contact with Kaan was a telephone call.

Fortunately Mrs Talbot took her side and insisted that Etta should stay to hear what Kaan had to say in person, even though it would clearly now mean staying overnight.

Mrs Trent left reluctantly, promising to return for her daughter early the next day.

'Thank you for showing me your beautiful house,' she said to Mrs Talbot as she left. 'My husband would love it.'

'You must bring him to see it sometime,' was the polite reply.

Mrs Trent left smiling and Etta realised that her parent went without too much protest because she had been given the perfect excuse to return.

'Now we just have to wait for Kaan to come back,' announced his mother. 'I wish he'd at least phone, but I expect he'll appear at any time now.'

The hours of waiting dragged by slowly, and in fact it was not until they were finishing dinner and the sun was sinking over the Bosphorus that the telephone rang.

Mrs Talbot pounced on it. 'Kaan? Where are you? I expected you hours ago.' She frowned at her son's reply, then nodded. 'Etta is staying here tonight,' she informed him.

Etta half-rose, ready to take the phone and speak to Kaan, but Mrs Talbot had already cut the connection. 'It appears we won't see him before bedtime,' she said with annoyance.

Etta retreated to her luxurious bedroom, convinced that she would not sleep a wink. She was going to stay awake, and the moment she heard Kaan arrive, she would be out of her room to greet him. Of course she didn't need sleep!

In fact she was fast asleep within ten minutes and didn't wake up until eight in the morning.

★   ★   ★

Etta found everything she needed in the adjoining bathroom from toothbrush to bath salts and now she soaked for some

299

time in a deep, hot, perfumed bath before reluctantly getting out and wrapping herself in an enormous, thick towelling robe.

It was a pleasant contrast to all the quick showers of the past few days. Peering at her wrist, she saw that an impressive bruise had formed there already, and she could see bruises ripening on her legs where she must have banged them against cars. When she went back into the bedroom she found that her case from the coach had appeared. Although these were the clothes she had planned to throw away, she managed to find some clean garments so that at least she looked reasonably presentable when she finally made her way to the dining room, where she found Mrs Talbot enjoying a leisurely cup of coffee.

'Is there any news of Kaan?' she asked eagerly after greeting her hostess politely.

'He's here,' was the surprising reply.

Etta glanced eagerly around as if

expecting him to appear from behind a chair. His mother laughed.

'I mean he's here — at home. In fact he's fast asleep in his room, next to yours. He woke me up when he got home in the early hours and promised to tell us everything once he'd caught up on his sleep.'

'How did he look?'

'He looked tired and his clothes were all crumpled, but he seemed happy enough. I don't think he's brought bad news. Now, if you'll excuse me, my dear, I've some work in my office.'

Left by herself, Etta breakfasted and then wondered what she could do with herself while they waited for Kaan to wake up. She wandered through the rooms, investigated the garden, then came back indoors with the intention of repacking her bag.

Outside Kaan's room she paused and put her ear close to the door, but she could hear nothing. She found herself gently turning the handle and pushing until there was a gap big enough for her to slip into the room.

It was in semi-darkness. Etta moved silently to the bed and looked down at Kaan, who lay on his back with his head turned to one side, sleeping deeply. She marvelled at the clean line of his cheek and jaw, aware of an almost overpowering urge to lie down beside him and hold his sleeping body in her arms.

'He looks very peaceful,' came a whisper. In spite of her size, Mrs Talbot had moved into the room very quietly, and now the two stood together. Kaan stirred, muttered, and turned on his side before Mrs Talbot led Etta out of the room.

'I think he's about to wake up at last,' she said. 'Will you wait for him in the dining room?'

Embarrassed by being discovered in Kaan's room, but grateful to his mother for not commenting on it, Etta murmured her consent.

Mrs Talbot put her hand on Etta's arm. 'I want to know what my son has been doing just as much as you do, but we'll just have to wait. At least he's here now and he's safe.'

The emotion in these last words suddenly revealed the stress and anxiety that Mrs Talbot had been concealing so successfully.

In fact it was half an hour later when Kaan finally appeared. His damp hair showed that he had showered, and he had abandoned his customary black for blue jeans and a white and blue striped shirt, which made him look much younger.

He greeted Etta, shook his head at the sight of her bruised wrist, and then began on a very hearty breakfast.

'It was mostly cups of coffee at the police station,' he said apologetically, reaching for another roll.

'Your mother is waiting in her office,' Etta informed him.

He nodded and continued to eat until her patience snapped.

'Kaan, you don't need another croissant — you've already eaten enough for three men!'

He grinned and pushed his empty plate away. 'Very well. I think I can survive now.'

He led the way to his mother's office, a large, airy room painted white, one wall lined with filing cabinets while a large window overlooking the Bosphorus almost filled the opposite wall. Mrs Talbot was seated behind a broad desk and she looked up eagerly as the couple came in, smiled a greeting, and waved them to two comfortable chairs facing her.

She leaned forward, elbows on the desk and her chin resting on her hands. Her gaze drilled into her son. 'So you're awake at last. They should not have kept you so long. I shall complain!'

Kaan laughed and shook his head. 'You wouldn't have been able to drag me away, Mother,' he told her. 'I refused to leave until I knew absolutely everything that had been going on!'

'And did you learn everything?' demanded Etta.

'I learned a lot, but there are still plenty of details which the police are working on.'

His mother held up a hand. 'Before you say any more, tell me quickly if this affair is going to affect Top Tours. Should I cancel the next group? If so, tell me now so that I can give as much notice as possible.'

Kaan shook his head. 'Certainly not. If it hadn't been for Etta's sharp eyes, nothing would have been found out. The police are very grateful to us and it won't affect Top Turkish Tours at all.'

His mother gave a sigh of relief. 'Now tell us everything.'

Kaan looked from his mother to Etta's expectant face, and drew a deep breath.

'Well, you know about that scene at the check-in desk. After that, Burke, Hunt and Trowbridge were all hauled off to the police office at the airport, and I was told to go along as well. I think the security guards thought at first that it was just a case of

Englishmen who'd had a bit too much to drink while they were waiting to be taken to the airport. Trowbridge kept on saying that he shouldn't be there, that it was nothing to do with him.'

He paused. 'Then finally they opened the shoulder bag, with Hunt protesting like mad that they had no right to do so and were invading his privacy. I was sure it would be just toiletries, travel documents and perhaps something he was ashamed of, like a dirty book or some photographs, and we'd all look fools.' He paused dramatically while the two women looked at him expectantly. The strain was too much for Etta.

'Go on, Kaan, before I hit you!' she almost snarled.

'There was a pair of dirty socks on top and my heart sank. I was trying to think how I could smooth over the situation. I knew the three of them would have missed their plane and I was trying to think how I could arrange seats on another flight. But then a policeman lifted the socks up and shook them, and out tumbled a fortune in jewels! They were just unmounted stones — diamonds, emeralds, rubies — but the size of them alone was impressive, and there were a lot of them.

'We all looked at Hunt, of course, but he'd gone absolutely silent, and so had Burke, so next the police took out what looked like a couple of books, but when they opened them they found that most of the pages had been cut away and those that were left were interleaved with banknotes — big denominations of all different currencies.

'After that, of course, the airport police decided that it was clear the matter was beyond their jurisdiction and needed serious enquiries. The police shut the three of them in a cell with a couple of armed guards and after a while we were all taken out and put in a police van and taken to police headquarters. Trowbridge was still protesting his innocence and the other two wouldn't answer any questions, so they were locked up separately while I had to tell the police all I knew.

'Then it was a case of examining everything else in the shoulder bag and then waiting while various places were contacted and enquiries made. After some hours they had a fairly good idea of what had been going on, so they brought the three men in together and the police told them that what they'd found out was enough to get all of them in deep trouble.

'At this point Hunt nearly collapsed and said he was willing to tell everything he knew. You should have seen how the other two reacted! They launched themselves at him before the police could stop them and tried to beat him unconscious before they were pulled off.'

'Trowbridge as well?'

'By then it was clear that Trowbridge was deeply involved.'

'What did Hunt tell you?'

He answered with another question. 'Do you remember how many big robberies there were while we have been touring? I joked once that we would end up as suspects. Well, I was right.'

Mrs Talbot's voice was full of horror. 'You mean our clients were robbers?'

'Not quite, Mother. Local gangs carried out the actual robberies. The problem with such robberies, however, is getting rid of the loot. Our friends bought the stolen goods with cash they'd smuggled into the country, then got rid of most of the stuff at other places we stopped at by selling it to crooked dealers. The further we were from the place where the actual robbery took place, the less chance there was of the jewellery being recognised.'

He turned to Etta. 'You were right about it not being Hunt's original shoulder-bag. Apparently the gangs would have the goods ready in identical bags so they could make the exchanges very easily and rapidly, but unfortunately for them the last gang had a bag with different coloured piping, as you noticed. That bag, the one they were taking out of the country, had some extremely valuable contents indeed.

'Of course, once it was known that they were linked to the robberies, the police wanted to know who their contacts were. Trowbridge wouldn't speak, but Hunt, and then Burke, were pouring out information. I've never seen such happy police! By now most of the robbers should have been found and arrested.'

A sharp movement by Etta drew his attention.

'What is it?'

'I didn't get round to telling you,' she said slowly, 'but Trowbridge sounded me out about travel reps acting as couriers and taking stuff from one place to another. He said it could be very profitable . . . '

Kaan's eyebrows rose. 'Did he, indeed? That's an interesting piece of information which I shall pass on to the authorities. They can check which companies Trowbridge has travelled with on previous trips to Turkey.'

Mrs Talbot sighed noisily. 'Well, I'm glad they've been caught, and that we helped to catch them. Now, while I get on with some work perhaps you'd like to show Etta round our house and garden. She hasn't seen them properly yet.'

But Kaan was holding up his hand. 'Wait! I haven't finished yet,' he said. 'As well as the money and jewels, there were several CDs which looked like albums by various singers, but in fact there were computer disks concealed in the CD sleeves and it was when the police checked their contents that things got really, really serious.

'You know, Etta, that Turkey has borders with a number of countries. Apparently these disks were from various dissident and terrorist groups, and as well as details of their organisations and members, there was also information about the activities they were planning for the near future.'

He laughed. 'After that we had half

311

the high-ranking police in Turkey at the station, as well as people from the security forces and the army. It all got very exciting. Our three friends won't be going back in England for a very long time.'

'What was David Trowbridge there for, if Hunt and Burke were actually collecting and carrying the stuff?'

'He was the head man. He contacted people and arranged the deals. Hunt and Burke were just couriers with muscle.'

'So all these high-powered people are going to feel indebted to us,' Mrs Talbot said with satisfaction. 'If it hadn't been for you and Etta these men would be back in England by now, safe from detection. Now, please go. I really do have things to do.'

Obediently Kaan and Etta wandered out into the garden. Leaning on a low wall, Kaan obeyed his mother's orders and indicated some of the notable buildings lining the Bosphorus.

Etta tried to look as if she was paying

attention, but her mind was too full of other things. She became aware that Kaan had stopped talking and was frowning at her.

'I'm sorry,' she said hastily, 'I was thinking of those men. We spent days in close proximity to them, and I thought they were odd but I would never have guessed they were criminals.'

'They're all ruthless men. Burke and Hunt provided the muscle, but Trowbridge was their leader, the real brains.' He shifted uncomfortably. 'I know you were friendly with him, Etta. I'm sorry if the discovery of what he really is distresses you . . . '

'No, I'm not upset. I accepted his invitations because it was flattering to be asked by an apparently charming and sophisticated man, but I never felt at ease. I always felt he had some other purpose in mind when he was being nice to me.'

Kaan looked as if an unspoken question had been answered to his satisfaction.

'Etta, do you realise that for the first

time since we met we're alone together? No tourists, no waiters . . . I've been hoping to get you to myself like this because I wanted to talk to you . . . '

It was, of course, at this very minute as Etta looked up at him expectantly, that the quiet scene was destroyed.

'Uncle Kaan!' two shrill voices were yelling, and suddenly two small bodies erupted from inside the house and wrapped themselves around Kaan, almost knocking him over.

'Go gently, children. Your uncle's had a tiring time.'

The warning came from a woman of about thirty who had followed the two young boys. One look showed her resemblance to Kaan and Mrs Talbot. This had to be one of his sisters.

Kaan confirmed this when he had unwrapped his nephews' embraces. 'Etta, this is my sister Ruya Hinkins, and these two noisy little objects are her sons, John and Jeremy.'

He turned to his sister. 'I didn't know you were here.'

'We just arrived.'

In spite of wearing a loose-fitting sundress, Ruya Hinkins still managed to look extremely elegant as she came forward and took Etta's hands. 'So you are Etta! The girl who had to cope alone when Kaan managed to get himself hurt. And you're the one who exposed the baddies! Mother has given me a short version of the story, but I want all the details from you two.'

★　★　★

Now two staff were bringing sun-loungers and little tables out on to the terrace. Mrs Talbot appeared and soon they were all comfortably settled with trays of coffee and apple tea at hand. Etta learned that Ruya lived in England, but her husband had had to go away unexpectedly on business so she had seized the opportunity to visit her family in Istanbul.

'I chose a good time to come. I see from your head and Etta's bruises that exciting things have been happening.'

'You've missed the exciting part. Things will be quieter now.'

'Not with these two here!' Mrs Talbot interjected, happily cuddling her grandsons. 'But I like having the house full.'

The house grew even fuller a few minutes later when Etta's mother and George Trent arrived. They were welcomed like old friends and, once Mrs Trent had assured herself that Etta was indeed making a satisfactory recovery, the day seemed to become one long party.

At one comparatively quiet time, Etta found herself sitting next to Ruya, watching Kaan play some energetic game on the floor with John and Jeremy.

'He gets on well with your boys,' Etta observed.

'Indeed he does — and with our sister Anna's two girls. They live in America, you know.'

'I didn't, but then until the last couple of days I've known very little about him.'

Ruya giggled. 'While I know quite a lot about you. Kaan always sends me long emails when he's on tour, and this time he told me all about you.'

Etta looked at her with horror. 'Oh? I hope he wasn't too rude about me. I was completely useless when I got here.'

Ruya giggled again. 'He said you didn't know a thing — but he also said that he thought you would learn quickly.' There was mischief in her sideways glance at Etta. 'And he also said you were very pretty and he was looking forward to teaching you.'

'That was not the impression he gave me!'

'Of course not,' was the airy reply. 'But you did learn quickly, didn't you? He made sure of that!'

As the day drew on, it became clear that Mrs Trent expected Etta to go back to the yacht with them. Etta was reluctant to leave the beautiful house on the Bosphorus, but she no longer had an excuse to stay.

However, when Mrs Talbot realised that Etta was intending to leave, she protested loudly. 'I expected her to stay for at least a couple of days more. Kaan planned to take her sightseeing and sailing on the Bosphorus in our boat.'

Mrs Trent hesitated, and a look full of meaning passed between her and Mrs Talbot. There was a pause before Mrs Trent said, 'Well, she will be on the yacht with us for some time, so if you really don't mind her staying . . . '

'She is a very welcome guest,' Mrs Talbot said firmly. Etta felt surprisingly happy. At least one more day with Kaan!

★ ★ ★

By mid-evening the Trents had gone back to their yacht and John and Jeremy were being put to bed by their mother.

'Come out on the terrace again,' Kaan invited Etta. 'I want to show you something.'

318

She followed him, and then gasped with wonder as he waved an arm at the view. The sun had set and the reflection of the stars glimmered on the waters of the Bosphorus.

'It's so beautiful!'

Kaan nodded his agreement. 'I love this time — especially after a full day like today.'

They stood in silence admiring the starlight on the rippling water, and then Etta turned to her companion. 'Kaan, there's one thing I'd like to know, and it's not about the robberies, it's personal. You said you weren't interested in Allegra because you'd met someone else and that you'd tell me who she was after the tourists had left. Well, they've long gone and I think after the way I was battered by one of your clients I've earned the right to be nosey . . . who is she?'

Kaan's golden eyes were serious and intent. 'Haven't you guessed yet, Etta?'

'How could I? I haven't seen you with any other girl . . . '

'No, of course not. There is no other girl. It's you.'

For several seconds she found she could not speak and she saw him turn his head away as if to hide his feelings.

'I should have waited, let you get to know me better,' he said sadly. 'You don't have to say anything, or you can tell me that you see me as a friend, or think up any other way of letting me down gently. You can go back to your mother's yacht tomorrow morning and we'll never see each other again.'

Gently, tentatively, she stretched out a hand and touched his bare arm with her fingertips, thrilling to the feel of his warm skin. 'Yes, I'll go back to the yacht, but I'll find my prettiest dress, and come back here and refuse to go away — ever!'

He turned back, his eyes searching her face with hope and uncertainty shown in equal measure. 'Do you mean . . . do you care for me, too?'

'Kaan Talbot, you have been a slave-driver. You have forced me to

320

forget about myself and work harder than I've ever done before to keep strangers happy and satisfied. For years I've always been aware that if I didn't like what I was expected to do, I could escape by going back to my mother. You taught me that self-respect comes from learning to do the best you can and not taking the easy way out. In the beginning the last thing I would have called you was lovable, but somehow I found that I had indeed fallen in love with you.' She stopped, suddenly shy. 'Perhaps it's because of the way you look at me with those golden eyes of yours . . .'

He gave a slow, deep sigh and encircled her in his arms as she lifted her face for his kiss. When they finally drew apart, his face was glowing with happiness.

'I had hoped . . . ' he said a little shakily. 'But I thought I had antagonised you and that you were turning to Trowbridge for comfort.'

Etta ran her fingers through his thick,

dark hair. 'You know, I've been wanting to do that for a long time.'

He grinned wickedly, and seized her round the waist. 'Some time I'll tell you what I've been wanting to do.'

Suddenly Etta's smile faded. 'We've known each other less than two weeks . . . '

'And you're thinking of your parents — how they fell in love, sure it would last, and then it all went wrong. Don't worry, Etta, I'm not going to rush things. I'm looking forward to courting you, sending you flowers, taking you out, getting to know all about you and letting you learn everything about me. But I know already that in the end we will be sure of our love for each other.'

He frowned. 'But you're sailing away soon with your mother. You can't go now!'

Etta managed to laugh. 'Don't worry! I think plans have been changed. Our mothers are getting on extremely well and don't want to part yet. My mother is actually hoping that George can rent a villa near here for a time.'

For some time they stood without speaking, their arms around each other, content to be so close.

'You know,' Kaan murmured finally, 'that our mothers are going to be absolutely delighted.'

'Then that will be four happy people — no, five, including my stepfather. He'll be thoroughly relieved that Mother won't be spending so much time chasing around trying to find me a suitable husband — now that I've managed to find one all by myself.'

She stopped suddenly, realising too late what she had said, but Kaan laughed.

'Of course we are going to be married!' he told her. 'Our mothers will enjoy fighting over the wedding . . . whether it is to be in Turkey or England, the colour of the flowers and the size of the cake . . . but I think they'll both make sure it's a marvellous occasion.'

He smiled down at her. 'But we

won't mention weddings to them for a while, and when we do, we'll have to make sure we tell them both at the same time.'

He tightened his arms around her and murmured, 'But for now it's just the two of us — at last! — and I so want to kiss you again.'

THE END

Other titles in the
Linford Romance Library:

SOME EIGHTEEN SUMMERS

Lillie Holland

After eighteen years living a sheltered life as a vicar's daughter in Norfolk, Debbie Meredith takes work as a companion to the wealthy Mrs Caroline Dewbrey in Yorkshire. Travelling by train, she meets the handsome and charming Hugh Stacey. However, before long, Debbie is wondering why Mrs Dewbrey lavishes so much attention on her. And what of her son Alec's stance against her involvement with Hugh? Debbie then finds that she's just a pawn embroiled in a tragic vendetta . . .

THE GIRL FROM YESTERDAY

Teresa Ashby

Robert Ashton and Kate Gibson are a month away from their wedding. However, Robert's ex-wife Caroline turns up from Australia with a teenage daughter, Karen, who Robert knew nothing about. Then, as Caroline and Robert spend time together, they still seem to have feelings for one another, despite the fact that Jim, back in Australia, has asked Caroline to marry him. Now, Robert and Caroline must decide whether their futures lie with each other — or with Kate and Jim.

LOVERS NEVER LIE

Gael Morrison

Stacia Roberts has always played it safe, yet, longing for adventure, she travels to Greece expecting sunshine and excitement — and gets more than she'd ever bargained for. When strangers try to kill her, she suspects her fellow traveller Andrew Moore might be the enemy — but is he really a friend? Andrew blames himself for his wife's death. Then he falls in love with Stacia, vowing to keep her safe, a difficult task when he discovers she's an international thief.

A LOVE SO TRUE

Sheila Spencer-Smith

Marooned in a lonely Dales farmhouse, in blizzard conditions, on a fell-walking challenge is not Tania Selwood's idea of a perfect holiday — especially as her co-leader Jake Anderson clearly resents her input into the welfare of their young charges. She struggles to hide her growing feelings for him as she fights to convince him they should stay. Can the beauty of their surroundings work its magic on them and make them realise their future happiness lies with each other?

THE HEART OF THE MATTER

Margaret Mounsdon

After the award-winning screen-writer Dominic Talbot leaves his briefcase in the back of one of Georgia Jones's cabs, she ends up working as his personal on-set driver. Despite his apparent romantic entanglement with leading lady Belle Jeffreys, Georgia finds her heart warming towards him. However, trouble haunts the film set. Dominic scoffs at the notion of a curse — until a cameraman breaks a leg, a fire breaks out, and the leading man catches chicken-pox . . .